G IS FOR GAMES

Also by Alison Tyler

———

G IS FOR GAMES

EROTIC STORIES
EDITED BY ALISON TYLER

CLEIS PRESS

Published in the United States by Cleis Press Inc.,
P.O. Box 14697, San Francisco, California 94114.

Printed in the United States.
Cover design: Scott Idleman
Text design: Karen Quigg
Cleis Press logo art: Juana Alicia
First Edition.
10 9 8 7 6 5 4 3 2 1

ACKNOWLEDGMENTS

Gratitude goes to those Gorgeous Gals:
The Lust Bites Ladies
and SAM, always.

Sex is a body-contact sport. It is safe to watch but more fun to play.
—THOMAS SZASZ, M.D.

Having sex is like playing bridge. If you don't have a good partner, you'd better have a good hand.
—WOODY ALLEN

What a wicked game you play....
—CHRIS ISAAK

contents

INTRODUCTION: GETTING LUCKY

G AMBLING ISN'T SOMETHING I'm especially good at. Yet I do love a good bet, and I've been told that I have a poker face to be proud of. Sure, I adore the rush of the unexpected win, pulling in the pile of chips with glee. But truthfully, I'm not that bad of a loser. It's the excitement of playing that turns me on.

Maybe that's why I like stories about games so much. The give-and-take. The way a player can lose the upper hand in a heartbeat, as in Kristina Wright's savagely sexy "Seven Minutes in Heaven":

Getting tied up should be a prelude to good, kinky sex, not a drunken party game. Unfortunately, this was one party game that had gone horribly wrong. What had sounded like a good idea when they were all doing shots of tequila in the kitchen, laughing and brushing up against each other, seemed like a very, very bad idea when one was tied up and sitting in a dark closet. Tied up and blindfolded. Burke squirmed in the chair and tested his bonds.

No deal—they weren't budging.

Some games have rules only one player understands, as in Bonnie Dee's "Showtime":

I used to play a game that let me walk on the wild side without actually doing anything too wild. Although in my late twenties, when I put on my old high school uniform and pulled my hair into pigtails, I still looked enticingly illegal. I wore that classic pleated skirt with no panties underneath, slipped my patent-leather shoes on over white bobby socks, buttoned my white Oxford shirt over my braless breasts, and strolled down to the Blue Heron Theater, where the triple-X movies were shown....

In other games, the rules are created as the players go along, as in Brooke Stern's "Unfinished Business":

"It's your game, Sarah. I don't even know if you want to be real."

"I want to be real. I do."

"Then tell me why you're here."

"I can't talk about it, Alex. Just do it to me. Please just do it to me."

"Just do what, Sarah?"

Silence. The rules of the game were very strict. It was her move. Alex couldn't move for her.

And then, of course, there's something to be said for cheating, as in Sheila Dare's "Play Me":

She'd lost the game—she'd climaxed first. But he'd cheated. He'd broken the rules and touched her.

Opening her eyes, she said with a smile, "Looks like we're going to have to play for the best two out of three."

So get ready, get set...are you feeling lucky?

Then go....

XXX,

Alison Tyler

MADELYNNE ELLIS

NO LIMITS

REEN, RIGHT FOOT."

I edged my foot across the tacky plastic.

"No limits."

No limits? It was the first thing he said to me. Our arms were cunningly entwined at the time, my nose pressed up against his arse, and his lips level with my right knee. Colored plastic, stuck to our palms and feet, squeaked and sighed with our every move. We were the final pair in a Twister death match, and I for one was going for broke.

"No limits to *what* exactly?" I asked. How much strain my calf muscles could take in order to make this a victory for the girls? The naughty look in his shocking blue eyes suggested not. I suspected he had something far more risqué in mind. So possibly what he meant was that there were no limits to how big a spectacle he was prepared to make of us. Not that I was worried on that score. You don't play Twister in a short skirt and fishnets without weighing up the consequences first. I knew exactly how much I had on display, and he couldn't strip me naked with his eyes.

"Left hand, red."

His palm slithered down my inner thigh, wakening hungry nerve endings, en route to its destination, the colored circle by my foot.

Okay, make that no limits to how much of a conniving bastard he was prepared to be in order to win. Slapping his wandering hands away would mean taking my own off the mat. Bingo!—instant victory to him, as if I'd fall for that.

"Mind your paws," I hissed, instead.

He stuck out his little finger in response and traced it along the sensitive bit on the side of my foot just below the ankle. He couldn't know it was a sweet spot, but I shivered all the same and felt a spark leap right up my leg and into my groin. He did it again. This time my clit tingled with need, and heat seeped into my cheeks.

"Stop that!"

He grinned.

I contemplated taking a bite out of his behind. It *was* rather attractive, now that I considered it. Firm, squeezable, and just perfect for scoring tiger stripes on with my fingernails.

"Right foot, blue."

Ah, payback time. Now let's see how good your balance is, I thought wickedly.

Instead of taking the easy option and giving myself some breathing space, I moved in closer and slid a stocking-covered thigh beneath his chest. My skirt slid up my leg leaving him staring at the smooth pale expanse of skin between the fishnet and my thong.

Gratified, I watched him wobble in response. He puffed a breath upward across his face, which lifted his feathery blond fringe. Not bad. I'd managed to get a reaction without resorting to touch.

"Red. Left foot."

He swiveled on his right foot, turned, hit the circle—and suddenly we were face-to-face.

He stared into my eyes, with his Cupid's bow lips slightly parted, plump, soft, and ready to kiss. I watched entranced as he slowly licked his lips.

"Left foot, green."

I brought my other leg forward, locked my arms against their protests as they took most of my weight, and somehow managed to keep my bum aloft.

"Right hand, green."

The spinner was on speed dial.

He leaned forward over me. "Think you can hold it steady?" he asked.

"No sweat. Do your worst."

He laughed, dipped his head, and licked a bead of perspiration from my breast.

I swallowed as his tongue tip lit sparks inside my chest: my nipples steepled in response, distorting the stretch fabric of my top. I wanted more and strained upward, eager to feel the brush of his tongue against those sensitive peaks. I no longer cared that he was resorting to touch. I wanted more and I wanted it fast. I stretched upward, but he lifted

— 3 —

himself higher, out of reach. He was trembling, too, and when I gazed along the length of his supple body, there was no missing the pleasing bulge beneath his fly.

My body seemed to liquefy at the sight, leaving a damp patch on my black lace panties. I wondered if he could smell my heat, my lust. I wondered if he guessed how much I ached to touch him.

"Yellow. Left hand."

"No limits," I whispered as I moved. "When are you going to fuck me?"

He flicked his fringe out of his eyes with a shake of his head. "Once I've won."

I arched a plucked eyebrow. "You won't win."

"Left hand, blue."

He shifted his weight to one arm and cupped his hand behind my head. His lips brushed mine. They teased, promising so much, fluttering over the surface in a gentle caress. He sucked at my lower lip, holding me captive when what I wanted was something deeper, hotter, and more intrusive. This tease was only exaggerating my need. Then his hips descended and the delicious bulge beneath his zipper brushed against my stocking top. I teetered.

"Nearly," he whispered, lowering his hand.

Somehow, I managed to regain my balance.

"Right hand, blue."

Damn it! I was cornered. My only option was to place my hand on the circle he already occupied. That's not strictly legal, but I wasn't beyond bending the odd rule.

I stretched my fingers toward him and interlocked mine with his. He clasped me tight in response. We'd progressed from combatants to symbionts.

Suddenly, the crowd surged forward, screaming incentives and put-downs, encouragement and outrage. One drunken fool barreled into us.

I wobbled…my hand slipped. But even as I tumbled, he held on to me and we collapsed together, to the thunder of applause.

On the mat, still tangled, he slipped his hand between my thighs to cup my mons. A single finger wriggled beneath the lace of my pants and into my wet heat. But the touch was fleeting, lasting only moments, before he pulled me to my feet. Hand in hand, we bowed. As the crowd applauded our efforts, he brought his stealthy finger to his mouth and sucked. He was tasting me, and there was no mistaking the pleasure in his eyes as a result.

I tweaked the Twister dial with my toes and watched it spin. The colors blurred. I smiled. Our bout was declared void. But I knew that we were both winners and that there would be more than just hands and feet moving between us tonight.

CHEYENNE BLUE

Game, Set, and Match

ATHERINGS AT MY BROTHER'S HOUSE were always dull, and this barbecue promised to be the usual mundane crowd of jawing suburbanites. My brother and his equally dull wife lived in one of Melbourne's most mind-numbing suburbs, and any gathering they hosted was a boring cacophony of accountants, teachers, and housewives all clattering on about their kids. Not my scene at all. If it were up to me, I'd have spent my Sunday afternoon—the hottest day of the Melbourne summer so far—in my air-conditioned apartment exploring the possibilities of my new vibrator. But I had to go—it was his birthday and I'd promised.

I arrived late, grabbed a beer, and looked around. Same old, same old. I made a mental note of the whereabouts of a few people I wanted to avoid and went to sit in a quiet corner, waiting until I could grab my brother, give him his present, and get the hell out of there. Even in the shade of a large wattle, the sweat rolled off me in waves, soaking though my singlet and into the waistband of my shorts. With nothing better to do, I idly watched the guests.

I saw her almost immediately, and my gaydar gave a little ping. Hell, who am I kidding?—it leaped off the scale. I looked closer. She was younger than I was, maybe in her early twenties, and the sort of cool blonde preppy kid I normally avoid. She was wearing tennis whites—a fresh, newly pressed skirt and a sort of cute, bobsy little top. Her hair was pulled off her neck into a jaunty ponytail. I watched her chat to my niece's kindergarten teacher, a desultory conversation that had her eyes flitting around the backyard, looking for escape.

The second time her eyes swept over me, I stared back. Her gaze moved on, then snapped back as if it were on elastic. I chugged my beer, threw the can into my sis-in-law's banked rows of flowers and waited for her to approach.

It took, oh, two point six minutes. I had closed my eyes and was jerked up in my seat by the feel of an icy-cold tinnie rolling around the back of my neck.

"Need a beer?" she asked.

She moved in front of me, and her crotch was level with my eyes. The short tennis skirt swayed as she shifted, and her lean brown legs had the sort of glorious bowline to the inner thigh that I love. Curved and hollow. It always makes me want to rest my cheek there and savor the taste of things to come. This was no exception. I could see downy blonde hairs on her thigh, so fine they could be cobwebs.

"Yeah, thanks." I dragged my gaze from her legs and accepted the beer.

"I'm Pippa." She squatted down on the grass in front of me, and I could see her panties. White of course, to go with the tennis outfit. I could smell trouble, there in the salty waves coming off her cunt.

"Excuse the clothes," she continued. "I live next door, and I was going to play a set with my sister, but she changed her mind when she saw the free beer here."

"You have a court next door?" My interest was roused. Tennis is my game, too; I like the competition; the combination of skill, force— and of course the women in shorts. Martina Navratilova got a lot of dykes into the game; I'm no exception.

"I do. Not a very good one, but I don't care. I like a game."

"Me too." I chugged my beer, and stood. "Wanna play?"

She caught my double meaning, no doubt about that, but she didn't hesitate. Her eyes raked me from top to toe, taking in the singlet and baggy shorts. "You got shoes?"

"In the car. I'll get them."

"That house there," she said, jerking a thumb. "The court is at the back, behind the hedge. Very private. You can't see it from the road or from here."

Her meaning was obvious, and a tingle of arousal ran from my nipples to my cunt, as surely as if they were connected by a cord.

"Five minutes."

When I found the court, she was already there, practicing her serve. I watched for a moment, studying her long, loose swing and the way she threw the ball high, before pounding down on top of it. She was good. I picked up the spare racket leaning against the chair, walked to the opposite end, and bounced experimentally on the balls

— 9 —

of my feet. Pippa inclined her head and batted a slow ball at me. I corrected my stance and drove back a forehand down the tramlines. For a few minutes we rallied back and forth, warming up. She was a club player, that was obvious—good control and heavy topspin. Not too much power behind it. I was more rough-and-ready, somewhat wilder, but I had greater strength and occasional erratic flashes of brilliance.

We tossed for serve and she won. I nearly missed her first ball—I was watching how her skirt flipped up, showing her panties as she smashed down on the ball. My return went wide. Fifteen–love. I concentrated on the second point, and we fought a long rally. Her long brown legs flashed around, and her breasts jiggled with the force of her ground strokes. A distraction for sure, but I held my own, making her run. Fifteen–all.

For the next twenty minutes, we played with heavy concentration. I summoned the steel of my idol Martina and fought every point doggedly, my flashes of luck compensating for my erratic backhand. The sweat rolled, and my hair clung to my neck in damp spikes, but I kept fighting.

She was three-two up and we were changing ends when I made my move. She handed me the water bottle, but instead of taking it, I grasped her wrist and pulled her closer—close enough that I could see her dusky nipples underneath the white top.

Her smile was feline. "I didn't think you really wanted to play tennis."

In answer, I wrapped my arm around her neck, bringing her close. I could see and feel the sheen of dampness on her cheeks, her parted lips and heavy breath before I closed the gap and kissed her. The day may have been hot already, but when her lips touched mine, the temperature shot up by another few degrees. Her hands—tiny hands, I noticed now—anchored my head and our mouths crashed together, opening, tongues tangling.

Liquid her mouth and instantly liquid my cunt. Our hands explored her back, my shoulder, her waist, my breast. I dropped my head, seeking the curve of her neck and shoulder, pushing my face into the muscle, smelling fresh sweat and sunshine. My tongue lapped at her sun-warmed skin, salty like the sea.

Pippa tilted her head, letting me explore, encouraging me with small mumbles of pleasure. Her scent rolled off her, intoxicatingly female. I fancied I could smell her salty cunt, curling through the humid area.

The sun burned hot on the back of my neck, and the sweat ran in runnels down my thighs. My panties were damp, but that wasn't only the temperature. Taking my hand, Pippa lead me beyond the baseline to where the wattles dropped golden flower globes onto the ground. Here the hard court ended and the grass began—long grass, uncut and starting to whither with the fierceness of the Australian summer.

With a long look, she grasped the hem of her top with both hands and pulled it over her head. A plain white cotton bra hid firm breasts, heavy with wide dark nipples. I touched one with my fingertip, watching it instantly tighten. Her skirt dropped away, leaving her in those ridiculously frilly tennis panties.

Swiftly, I stripped off my own damp singlet and let my shorts drop to the ground. I never wear a bra—don't need one with my boyish chest—and my panties were plain, serviceable cotton. I kicked my clothes away.

She reached for me at the same instant as my hands sought her body. We sank to the ground, and my face was in her breasts as I palmed her nipple and bit gently on its partner. I had expected her to be more passive, more diffident in her approach to sex. The jaunty ponytail, the whole tennis thing had led me to expect that I would be the aggressor. But Pippa was fighting for the upper hand, trying to push me over onto my back so that she could feel my breasts.

For a moment, I gave way, and abruptly I found myself on my back with her astride me. Our panties touched and our thighs rubbed together. My palms smoothed her inner thighs, finding the curve I love so well. Her fingers rubbed my nipples and I sighed in pleasure, closing my eyes against the bright sunlight that filtered through the trees. When her hand crept under my panties, I raised my hips, encouraging her to remove them. She took the hint, and immediately her fingers were there, sliding over the lips, then dipping inside. Pippa shifted, lying between my spread thighs; one finger, two, then three slipping slowly in and out, sliding easily in the moisture, curling around, pressing up, stretching me, finding my G-spot with easy skill. She pistoned fast, fucking me with her small hand, a welcome penetration. When her thumb passed over my clit, the spasms started, intensified, and burst in a rolling golden wave of pleasure. My back arched from the ground, and my mouth opened in a soundless scream.

When the spasms eased, I became aware of our surroundings, the dry grass stalks in my back, the shrill of the cicadas. Pippa raised up and pressed her fingers to my lips, forcing me to taste my juices. I allowed it for a minute, while my breathing slowed, steadied, and then I pushed her hand away.

My turn.

Still on my back, I encouraged her forward, guiding her thighs so that they settled on either side of my head. Turning, I pressed a kiss against their lean curve. Her panties were gone, kicked away to lie in the grass. Instead, there was her bare pussy inches from my mouth, covered with downy blonde hair, musky with the scent of summer. I learned her with my fingertips, tracing the lines of her lips, feeling the texture of her moisture. And then, when the longing became too much, I tasted her, savoring the starburst of her cunt on my tongue. I was gentler than she had been; I lapped with short, gentle strokes, then pushed my tongue in deep, seeking paradise.

Pippa's thighs clenched about my head, clamping on my ears so much that the pressure created an artificial sea-murmur in my ears. Her hair had worked loose from the ponytail and curled in damp tendrils against her neck. But I didn't let her come. As she worked up to her peak, as her moisture flowed freely over my mouth and chin, I eased back and pushed her off my face, an abrupt motion that had her sprawling in the grass. She stared up at me, the sex-flush spreading down over her pale breasts.

I parted her legs and reached for the tennis racket. The handle was worn smooth from years of sweat and firm grip, and it was fat and hard. I eased it into her cunt, letting her relax around the intrusion. Then, letting it rest, I put my mouth back down to her snatch again. This time, I kept going, tonguing her hard, lashing her shivering clit with long, wet strokes. When she came, the racket quivered in her cunt, trembling against the side of my face. I pulled it out and handed it to her. Her fingers closed around the grip, and she mimed an imaginary backhand slice.

"I think this racket's just played its best match," she murmured.

Her sleepy, cat-slit eyes told it all. I rested my head down again onto her thigh and let my fingers tangle in her soft pubes.

My words vibrated against her skin. "Fancy a rematch sometime?"

ERICA DUMAS

THE BIG TOUCHDOWN

GREAT," YOU SAY, pulling the station wagon in at the top of the point, into a parking place shrouded by trees. "The perfect spot."

There's no view from here, but it doesn't matter; we're not going to be looking. The only lights are angled shafts from one faraway klieg light. We get into the backseat and start to make out. From the second our lips touch I can feel your cock growing in your blue jeans. Our tongues intertwine as I slip my hand under your football jersey and stroke your muscled chest.

"Ohmigod," I say enthusiastically, "I couldn't believe it! That was *so* great when you caught the pass and ran fifty yards for the big touch-down!"

"Yeah?" you say, smiling, all arrogant and pleased with yourself.

I giggle. "Yeah! I was sooooo proud of you!"

You kiss me, hard, your tongue deep in my mouth as your hand touches the swell of my breast under the tight poly-cotton cheerleader uniform. Your palm gently presses my nipple as it stretches the fabric.

"Did it make you wet?" you ask with a wicked smile on your face.

I look into your eyes and say breathlessly, "Yeah." Then, with a broad smile: "It made me want to suck you."

"That's what I like to hear," you say and lean back.

I can't resist it any longer. As you stretch out on the backseat, I lower myself and push my face against your crotch, feeling your cock swelling in your blue jeans. I whimper softly as I press my lips around your bulge, fumbling with your belt. You grab your buckle and unfasten it yourself, then unzip your pants, revealing your cock, outlined in white jockey shorts that seem to glow in the faint light. How does Mom get her whites so white? I wonder. I reach into your jockeys and pull out your hard cock. I lick the head, tasting your salty pre-come, then take your cock in my mouth and listen to you moan softly as I start to suck you off.

"You looked so good running through those routines," you say as my head bobs up and down in your lap. "I couldn't wait to get you alone after the game. Why do you think I ran so fast?"

My mouth slides off you and I beam up at you. "You're just saying that!"

"No, really." Your voice is hoarse. "If your ass hadn't looked so fine every time that skirt flew up, I wouldn't have been able to run like that. I couldn't wait to get a piece of it."

I giggle and slide your cock between my lips again, feeling my pussy surge with every thrust down. You're moaning again, a little louder, getting more excited as my hand works the shaft of your cock and my tongue circles the head. Your hands find the back of my cheer-leader jersey and unzip it, pulling it forward. I ease my arms out so you can reach down to stroke my breasts through my sports bra. When you pull it up, I moan louder. Your fingers stroke my nipples through the damp material. You're getting closer, your arousal mounting as I bring you nearer your orgasm with every swirl of my tongue.

You pull me off your cock, both of us panting.

"Kristi, please, just let me put it in a little," you beg.

I blush deeply. "Mi-i-ike!" I say, drawing your name out into three syllables.

"Please. I promise I won't come. I promise I'll go slow."

I'm panting hard now, my pussy throbbing so hard there's no way I could say no. But I play the game, looking up at you insistently.

I clutch the front of my jersey over my breasts. "You *promise*? You *promise* you won't come?"

You make an *X* over your chest. "Cross my heart and hope to die."

Looking up at you, I say, "All right. But just put it in a little."

You're on me in a flash, pushing me back into the seat, your mouth hot against mine, your tongue plunging deep into me. Your fingers slide up my skirt and down my gold and green regulation panties, the same color as my skirt. Your hand finds my pussy, and you know in an instant just how wet I am for you. Your finger slides into me easily, but I gasp as if it's a surprise to me. Then I moan softly and wriggle deeper into your grasp.

"Promise you'll go slow?" I beg.

"Promise," you say and claw at my panties, pulling them down my thighs. They peel away from my pussy all sticky and wet. I put my legs

— 17 —

up and you slide my panties over my ankles. You lean forward onto me and I spread my legs, leaning back as you lift my sports bra over my breasts.

Your mouth on them feels good, and I lie there running my fingers through your hair as you urgently tongue my nipples. I lift my hips slightly, and you reach down to guide your cock between my lips. I'm so wet you could drive into me with a single hard thrust. But still I say, "You promised. Go slow."

You slide into me gradually, the first wave of pleasure hitting me when your head pops into my cunt. My mouth opens wide and I gasp, wordless, inarticulate with the pleasure of your cock filling me. I don't want you to go slow: I want you to pound into me, fuck me so hard I scream. But I whisper, "Go…slow…Mike…. Please…go…slow…."

You obey, moaning against my breasts as you ease your cock in as deep as it will go. I wrap my legs around your body and pull you deeper into me.

"Is it all right?" you ask breathlessly.

"It's…good," I gasp. "It's…great."

You start to fuck me slowly, and I twist and writhe under you as I pull you harder onto me with my legs spread wide and curved around your hips. "You can do it harder," I whimper softly, and you begin to fuck me faster, pumping into me as I drag my fingernails across your back. I'm close, maybe closer than you are—but I'm not sure. That's why when I hear your breath quickening I moan softly, "Don't…come…. Don't…come…."

But it doesn't matter, because just saying it turns me on more, "Please don't come!" I beg as I hear your moans, your cock pulsing faster into me, and then I reach my orgasm, my legs tightening so firmly around yours that you stop thrusting and I beg, "Don't stop! Please don't stop!"

You start fucking me again, harder than ever, struggling against the uncontrolled tightening of my legs around you. Your cock feels huge as I tighten around the thrusting shaft, each spasm of my orgasm growing stronger as you fuck me. When my climax shudders to a halt, I pull you so firmly against my body with my legs that you stop thrusting again. I press your face between my hands and push your mouth to mine.

You start fucking me again, even harder this time, even faster. I untangle my legs from yours and spread my thighs wider. "Come inside me," I beg, moaning. "Shoot your come inside me."

You look nervous, unsure.

"It's all right," I sigh. "I want you to. Come inside me."

Your back arches, your head rolls back, and you moan as your cock pulses deep in my pussy. I can feel the wetness, drowning out even my own. "Yes, yes, yes," I sigh as you slump on top of me, and I caress your hair, kissing the side of your face. Your cock slides out of me, and I can feel the wetness of your come leaking out of my pussy, so dangerous, so taboo.

Still panting, you glance at your watch.

"What time do we have the babysitter till?" you whisper.

"Eleven," I say.

"It's ten thirty," you tell me. "We really ought to get going."

I nod and kiss you one more time. You climb off me and hunt for my panties, but they're hidden somewhere in the darkness of the back-seat. "Forget them," I tell you, and we both get into the front seat.

Before you start the car, I kiss you again, hard. "How does it feel to have made the big touchdown?" I whisper to you when our lips part.

"Great," you smile, "every single time," and then you turn the key.

SHEILA DARE

PLAY ME

GIVEN THAT SHE'D ONLY PLAYED STRIP POKER once back in high school, this should have set off more warning bells. Back then, she'd won the pot, then lost her virginity. This time the stakes seem far higher. High enough to give her vertigo.

After draining her white wine, she plunked her glass on the room-service cart and asked, "Who goes first?"

He dug a quarter from his pocket. "Flip for it?"

"Heads," she called. It came up tails.

He smiled. A lazy smile that had her throat tightening. He walked back to his chair, sat down, wine in his hand, eyes glittering and eager.

Her mind blanked. She glanced around the hotel room.

What was she doing here? This was business, and he was supposed to be the competition for a prime account. But sharing a cab back from LidoSoft's corporate offices had led to sharing dinner and war stories of the last time they'd met to duel in business. Then to after-dinner drinks in his hotel room and this bet.

"You want the LidoSoft account, don't you? Badly?" he'd asked, voice smooth, sexy mid-Atlantic Brit at its best.

She'd stared at him, toyed with a strand of dark hair that brushed her shoulder, then tucked it behind her ear. "And you don't?"

He shrugged. He'd taken off his jacket, pulled his tie loose. He looked better like this—rumpled, accessible, and without pin-striped gray hiding the lean muscle of him. What was it about a rolled-up, white shirt cuff on a man?

"It'd be a nice morsel," he said. "But it's not even an appetizer for a company like BGG."

She'd given him a look over her wineglass that said, *Sure, sweet stuff, tell me another.* But she knew it was the truth. An ad agency the size of BGG didn't need LidoSoft. She and her brother did.

He only smiled. Then he said, "It's a dangerous competition we have going. Care to make it even more interesting?"

She'd pulled in a breath, known she ought to make a joke and head back to her room. Only she'd feel a hick. And she'd shaken off the dust of small-town Nebraska for the big city years ago. Reckless with wine, she said she was game.

Now she lifted her powder-blue skirt, eased it over the tops of her thigh-highs, and wondered just whose game this was. His gaze flickered to her legs. Locked there. His hand tightened around his wineglass. Heady stuff to keep a man's eyes on you like that. To keep his eyes there—the top man at the top agency in the country. Her breathing quickened. She liked the rush of this. She liked these wicked rules.

Pure, raw daring lifted her pulse.

She looked down at herself. Wet her lips. *Could she really do this?*

Inching the skirt higher, she let her fingertips brush the black lace that topped her thigh-highs. Then she looked at him.

"I hate panty hose."

Glassy-eyed, he nodded, then said, "Sign me up and we'll start a movement against them."

That voice—throaty with lust—pulled another flash of heat from her. She wet her lips with the tip of her tongue, kept lifting the skirt.

She'd worn black lace. A skimp of it. Now she ran her fingers over the front, touching dampness.

"Don't like underwear much, either," she said, and slid the black lace down, letting her skirt fall back into place as well.

His stare flashed to her face. Aroused. Excited. But not shocked. Not startled. Still far too together.

She'd have to do better.

Hands fumbling, she started with the buttons on her blouse, keeping her stare fixed on them as she undid them. The bra matched the undies. Cream silk undone, she looked at him. He'd drained his wine. The glass lay in loose fingers.

She set her mouth.

She'd nail him. She'd see him, head back, moaning, eyes lost to passion. She'd have him lose his cool—and the game. For once, she was going to go up against him and win.

Pulling her skirt high, she lifted it to her waist, then stepped wide, spreading her legs like a hooker out to entice a paying client. She'd never done anything like this. Heaven, but did it feel good! Powerful.

Freeing. Sexy as hell, and so bad it made her smile. Heart pounding, she wondered why she'd waited so long to be so bad.

Reaching down, she put one finger into the wet slickness between her legs, then spread the softness she found with her fingers. Her arousal filled the room like a hot sea. She wiggled her hips and looked at him. "Like it?"

He nodded as if she'd stolen his words and he couldn't find them again. She could see an interesting bulge lift the front of his gray trousers. Could she make him so wild he dragged her onto the floor and slammed into her, velvet hard and sweetly hot? But no—not the time to go there now. This was about winning. About making him lose it.

She pushed two fingers into wet warmth.

The pulse jumped in his throat. It pounded in her.

Eyes drifting closed, she turned, leaned a hand on the bed, gave him a show of her ass and the view from behind. She kept her fingers rubbing, slipping in and out again. Heat washed over her, through her. Her eyes closed with raw pleasure. Closed with the excitement of him watching.

His stare pushed her on.

Leaning on the bed, she wiggled again for him. Spread her legs wider. Made it easy for him to see. She could see, too. In the mirror behind him. Thighs white above black stockings. Lace tickling round cheeks. Powder-blue skirt bunched around her waist. Pink lips parted and moist. She'd never felt so hot. So wet. So turned on.

Sighing, low, deep, she rubbed. Faster now.

Her hips jerked as a moan slipped out. She gave in to the heat. Just her and her fingers. She knew how to do this, how to do herself. But having him watch. Bad, oh, bad, oh, so very good.

Opening her eyes, she watched him.

He had his hand on his trousers, palm pressing down. Her breath quickened. She was close to the edge, but that would lose her the game. So she straightened, turned, and sat on the bed.

Time to crank up the heat.

Gulping down a breath, she brought wet fingers up and pulled off her blouse. She pulled in a breath and the scent of sex that drugged the air. Slipping silk off her shoulders, she smiled. Air conditioning slid over her skin and the room smelled like hot need. Tugging her bra down, she left it fastened so it pushed up her breasts, kept them lifted and begging for his touch.

"Do you know what I really like?" she asked. She wanted to giggle. She wanted to tear off her clothes, tell him to forget the game, and find a good seat across his lap.

But rules were rules.

And she wanted to win.

Slowly, eyes glazed, he shook his head.

His eyes flickered to hers and then to her breasts, locking there as if he thought they held the secrets of the universe.

She took one breast in each hand, took the hard tips between thumb and forefinger. It must be that wine of his. Or that bod of his—all lean muscle and elegant accent. Or maybe it was just him—the man she'd lusted after for far too long in secret dreams she'd never admitted to anyone.

"What I really like," she said, voice raspy and thick, the way she'd always wanted to sound and never had, "is a guy with a bite to him."

She pinched the tips of her breasts. Hard.

She almost had him there. Saw it in the jerk of his hand, the hot flare in widening eyes, the tension knotting his shoulders.

Smiling, her eyes shut as she let herself go for it. Let her slicked fingers roll on hard nipples even as she thought about having his hands on her instead.

"I could play with them all day. I have, you know. I've gone into the bathroom at work"—such a lie—"and locked the door, and undone my blouse like this, and then rubbed and squeezed and pinched. I have these things I bought. From a catalogue. With little clamps—they're vibrators." That was true. "They're not like a man's teeth. Not as good. But I pretend."

She tugged. Pulled. Put her head back and moaned at how good it felt. Then she looked at him.

And the sight of him—lips parted, eyes glazed, hand holding back that thick bulge in his trousers—just about had her losing it.

Stare locked on him, pulse quick and hard in her throat, she kept at him. "I pretend it's your mouth on them."

That broke him. His stare jerked to her face, then he launched out of the chair and across the room at her.

His mouth wrapped over her fingers. She threw her head back as his mouth found the place she most wanted it to be and lightning arced into her. He leaned her back, his hips pressed against her thigh. She pulled her hand away and pressed more of her breast into that hot, hungry mouth.

He lifted up, loomed over her, eyes dark. Then dragged off his shirt, buttons popping. She blinked. She'd never had a guy ruin a shirt for her.

Gaze roaming, hands following after, she took in the hard muscles of his chest, the dusting of dark hair spread across his pecs, the firm, tan skin.

"It's a sin to ever put you in a suit," she said.

He grinned. Then pushed her breasts together and took both pink tips in his mouth. She gasped and squirmed as he tormented. She bucked as he bit down.

Soft, then hard.

So amazingly hard she lost it.

Lights burst behind her eyes. Exploded as muscles clenched. The world tightened to searing, delicious sensation. She rubbed against him, wished she had him filling her. Instead, he sucked harder. She arched to him, body pulsing, muscles contracting as her hips jerked and she went over the edge.

She'd lost the game—she'd climaxed first. But he'd cheated. He'd broken the rules and touched her.

Opening her eyes, she said with a smile, "Looks like we're going to have to play for the best two out of three."

JOEL A. NICHOLS

THINK OF BASEBALL

GRINDING HIS TONGUE INTO HER, Rick Sullivan mouth-fucked his wife. It was something he knew he had to do, and he wanted to do it better than her friends' husbands. He knew they talked about it and hoped that Callie was the happiest. He licked her pussy lips, pushing them apart with the blade of his tongue. She tasted salty and wet, and each new slick of her juice coating his chin was hotter than the last. Wispy pubic hair tickled his nose as he lapped at her. She squirmed around beneath his face, flexing and bending her hips and ass as he electrified her cunt.

For most guys, thinking about baseball would slow them down with their wives. Rick had to think about mowing the lawn. If he thought about the game, he shot right away, at the bottom of the first. He wanted to last as long as he could, wanted her to come every time, so she didn't think anything was wrong with their sex life.

Rick licked his index finger and ran it up her thigh, slipping it inside her as he nibbled her lips and flicked his tongue at her clit. Callie moaned and spread her legs. Rick rocked from side to side as she dug her pink toenails into his waist, and then buried his whole face in her. He finger-fucked her slit and kept tonguing, licking his own finger as it disappeared into her. Every few beats he pinned her clit down with the tip of his tongue, thinking about the princess and the pea, and stroked it feather-light. She grabbed a handful of his hair and yanked him off her pussy.

"I want you to fuck me," she said, letting go of his head and leaning back on the pillows. Rick's scalp burned.

She lifted her knees and reached down to guide his cock into her. He was huge—too huge to wear swim trunks in the summer because he invariably fell out the leg hole of the longest trunks—and even when she was already relaxed and aroused from his mouth and fingers, she always grasped him and fed him into herself slowly. But after that first stroke, Callie left it up to him. She squeezed her eyes shut and felt him fill her up. Rising against his hips, she welcomed his girth from the inside with hot, moist friction. Rick leaned over her and nuzzled her neck, biting her earlobe as his weight fell over her chest. Her nipples were hard against him, her breasts warm against his hairy chest.

He drilled her, over and over. She was breathing heavily and wet flooded her thighs. It was always like that when she was getting close, when Rick was sure that he was hitting all her spots. He felt himself lagging and reached down. He grabbed his balls, then jerked the bottom of his dick. His cockhead was still buried inside her as he pumped the bottom. Callie pressed her fingertips over her clit and bore down with her legs, gripping him tight. She moaned, driving her fingertips into his thigh. "Harder," she growled, tugging at his hip. "Fuck me harder. Now. Harder." The last syllable disappeared in a gasp.

Rick let go of his dick and slid it all the way in her. His balls smacked against her ass. His knees started to burn, and another wave of wet sluiced out of Callie. Her head was thrown back and the corners of her lips curved up. They pounded away at each other until a damp sheen of sweat covered them both. She started to come again, grasped his hips with both hands and pulled him into her. She let loose a gasping moan.

Rick bit down on his lip and pretended to come, bucking his hips, grinding them into his wife. He said, "Fuck, yeah" and "I love you." He pushed his cock all the way in and shook, pumping an imaginary load deep in her.

"Holy…" Callie said, trying to catch her breath. "It feels like I'm floating," she whispered. They mashed their lips together and deep-kissed. Rick rolled onto his stomach to hide his hard-on and threw an arm over her breasts. Callie's eyelids fell shut. Her cheeks were still pink with the flush of orgasm as Rick rolled on top of his big cock. The pressure he'd built up wouldn't go away until he could stroke it out, and he never could with her. When her breathing was regular, Rick stole out of bed, his hard-on still red and stiff. It pointed his way out through the breezeway and into the garage.

Rick had played second base in high school and shortstop in junior college. Coaches were always impressed by his hard work and quick legs. He was a good catcher and a not-bad hitter. His team plaques hung on the wall of the garage, team photos stretching back to Little League. In every one of those group pictures, Rick was easy to pick out: the redhead with a sideways smile.

Rick had a big, red, metal toolbox tucked against the wall with all the memorabilia. The heat of his cock warmed his thighs in the cool garage. It was still wet with her juice and jutted out from his tight belly. Above the toolbox hung a varnished baseball bat all the teammates had signed at graduation. Matt Deichman had signed right at the top, ringing the thick end with a bad-boy scrawl. Deichman had been the first baseman. Rick closed his eyes and remembered watching him watch the batter. It was the best part of baseball that year, for Rick: he had to keep his eyes on Matt Deichman because that's always where the ball was going to come from.

Even back then his cock would start to fill up inside his tight jock. And when he thought of standing in red dirt, waiting for Deichman's move, he felt a low ache in his balls, a missing piece of pleasure.

He stroked himself slowly, shaking his big dick from the bottom and letting its weight make it harder. The first times he'd gone out to the garage in a bathrobe, afraid that his wife would catch him. But he knew she never woke in the night, especially after he'd fucked her like that. Rick reached up and hefted the baseball bat off its hooks. He rubbed the circular ridge at the bottom against his cock, which slicked a wet trail on the smooth and cool wood. He smacked it against his stomach a couple of times and his cock was back to full girth, red and pulsing hot.

With perfectly squared shoulders, Rick took two shadow swings. As he released his elbows and arched into the ideal hyperextension, his dick thudded first against his right thigh and then rebounded against his left. Whenever jealous guys in the locker room razzed him about his meat that was long even when it was soft as dough, Deichman never said anything. Sometimes a blushing Rick would watch to see his reaction when they started up, but Deichman never raised an eyebrow. Rick knew from watching out of the corner of his eye in the shower that Deichman's dick wasn't nearly so hefty.

He hit imaginary homers, and swing after swing his dick slapped against his thighs and belly. In the night cool, his nipples stood hard and goose pimples rose on his naked chest and legs. After a few more practice hits, he tipped the bat down, aiming the thick end at the floor of the garage. He ran it along the length of his cock. At the blunt end— where Deichman's name lay in black marker—the bat dwarfed his dick. But as he slid the two shafts along each other, Rick's meat gained ground on the bat. It was thicker than the handhold and felt just as heavy as the varnished wood.

Rick spit in his hand and wrapped his palms around his dick and the narrow end of the bat. It took both hands to reach around the shafts, and Rick sighed as he squeezed his thick cock up against the bat. The contrast between the fire of his skin and the inner cool of the wood made his balls grow tight, and he moved the bat like a joystick.

As he stroked, he imagined that the bat was Deichman's hard-on. It was something he'd seen in one of the fag rags he kept hidden at the bottom of the toolbox: a porno dude jerking himself and somebody else at the same time, struggling to wrap his fingers around that much cock. Rick closed his eyes and pumped away with both hands, feeling a tightening in his balls.

The bat slipped from his grasp and clattered to the cement floor. Rick stood stock-still for two breaths, listening for his wife's footfalls from their bedroom, his hand a vise around the base of his flagging dick. After those beats of silence, he whacked it into his damp, open palm. It made a wet crack, and at both the friction of the slaps and the sound, his dick flared again. By now he'd been hard for almost an hour, and he was starting the feel the fluttering in his chest as his heart struggled to beat enough blood into his massive tool.

He squeezed the skin up around the base of his shaft. Spitting into his hand again, he slicked the crown of his cock and started pumping his fist with long, even strokes. After a few seconds, he bent over and picked up the bat. He balls hung heavy in the open air. This time Rick held the baseball bat at the blunt end. He crouched and straddled the bat, grinding the narrow end into the cement. He eased the end where Deichman had scribbled his name underneath his balls and leaned into it, letting the pressure build against that thin strip of skin between his ass and his balls.

Rick rode the bat, squeezing it between his asscheeks. His face and body flooded with heat as he imagined for a second crouching over Deichman, imagined the baseman's dick playing at the edges of his ass. Rick clenched and unclenched as he stroked himself, making the image disappear and pulling his length through his slick fist. He licked his thumb and slid it around the ridge of his cockhead.

Deep inside his balls and ass, the pressure built and he leaned into the bat standing smooth and hard against his asshole. He beat his cock two-fisted, smacking it against his palms and kneading it up and down, up and down. The floor of the garage was cool along the burning soles of his feet. Rick flexed his legs, opening up his ass in the night air. He gave one last hard push against the blunt end of the baseball bat and his spine lit on fire, a rolling ball of heat that uncoiled from inside him and floated across the surface of his skin in a wave of pinpricks.

The bat clattered to the garage floor as Rick grunted and started to explode. His knees shook as the last surge of orgasm crested. With weak limbs, he bent and picked up the heavy baseball bat. He palmed the slick blunt end, rubbing his wetness into the varnished wood. He took one last look at Deichman's signature, then hung the bat back on the hooks next to the rows of photographs. Then he followed the breezeway into the house, padded through the kitchen and into the bedroom. He slipped in next to his wife, curled up next to her, and collapsed into sleep.

KRISTINA WRIGHT

SEVEN MINUTES IN HEAVEN

G ETTING TIED UP SHOULD BE A PRELUDE to good, kinky sex, not a drunken party game. Unfortunately, this was one party game that had gone horribly wrong. What had sounded like a good idea when they were all doing shots of tequila in the kitchen, laughing and brushing up against each other, seemed like a very, very bad idea when one was tied up and sitting in a dark closet. Tied up and blindfolded. Burke squirmed in the chair and tested his bonds.

No deal—they weren't budging.

He could hear his girlfriend Caroline's laughter on the other side of the door. She was three sheets to the wind and feeling horny. He could tell because when she closed the closet door on him, she had said, "Don't worry. I'll be the one to finish you off."

He groaned. *Finish him off.* At the time, he'd thought she meant sexual release. Now he was thinking execution. He strained against the ties around his wrists. And they *were* ties, *his* ties. Ties that had been hanging in the bedroom closet but were now wrapped around his wrists in the hall closet. Wrapped tight, too. Caroline sure knew how to tie a mean knot.

The fact that she wanted him tied down and helpless didn't bother him. What bothered him was that she intended to send her friends into the closet, one by one. Which wouldn't even be so bad, except that two of the six people in the living room were guys. Burke, despite some drunken experimentation during college, was very much straight. The fact that he couldn't see anything, even when the door opened, only made things worse. He was pretty sure he'd know a guy's touch from a girl's, but he didn't like feeling this damned helpless.

His cock, on the other hand, didn't seem to mind at all. It was standing at attention, or as much at attention as it could while he was clothed and sitting down. He shifted uncomfortably, with hopes of adjusting, rather than freeing, himself. He groaned in frustration.

"Wait for me, baby," a female voice purred.

He hadn't heard the closet door open and he couldn't tell if it was closed. Were they watching? No, that wasn't how the game was played. Seven Minutes in Heaven was played with the door closed so no one outside the closet knew what was going on inside the closet. It was cold comfort, under the circumstances.

He felt a soft, feminine hand on his face. He was pretty sure it was Natalie, Caroline's best friend from college. Burke didn't know Natalie very well. Hell, he didn't know any of Caroline's friends very well. That's what this little party was all about. Now that they were living together, Caroline wanted him to get to know her friends better. This wasn't quite what he had in mind.

"I'll go easy on you, sugar."

The voice was a sweet, feminine Southern drawl. It had to be Natalie, though his first impression of her had been anything but sweet. She had a bit of a hard, aloof edge to her. Or so he thought. She seemed anything but aloof as she ran her fingers through his hair and bent down to nibble on his earlobe.

"Natalie, right?" he croaked, trying desperately for some levity even while his cock threatened to rip through his jeans. Why was this turning him on so much?

"Right, sugar," she breathed in his ear, rimming it with the tip of her tongue. "Nervous?"

He laughed. "A little. This is an unusual getting-to-know-you strategy."

"Don't worry, Caroline gave us some ground rules." Her laugh was low and sultry. "We'll be good. Well, as good as we have to be."

Burke realized he was leaning into her lips, willing her to nibble down his neck. "What ground rules?"

Taking the hint, she slid her hands down to his shoulders and leaned in, nipping at his neck. "We can kiss and touch, but no actual sex is allowed. She just wants you hard and ready for her."

It wasn't great, but he'd been afraid he'd end up naked in here. He relaxed, allowing himself to enjoy Natalie's attention. She licked and sucked his neck for a couple of minutes, hard enough that he knew he'd have a mark or two to show for it. He wondered if Caroline had stacked the deck against him by telling her friends exactly how to drive him crazy.

"Oh yeah," she drawled, "I forgot. We can undress you, as much as your restraints will allow." She bit down on his neck. "Should I unzip your pants?"

"No, please," he said. He sounded breathless even to his own ears. "I'd rather keep my pants on."

Natalie laughed softly. "Your call, sugar. But at some point, those pants are going to get opened and Mr. Happy is going to come out to play."

The knock on the door startled them both.

"Time's up," Caroline called. "We have other people waiting."

Natalie ruffled his hair. "Thanks, sugar."

Burke only had a moment to relax before the closet door opened, Natalie left, and someone else joined him. The door closed with a decisive snap and female giggling.

"Hi, Burke."

Burke recognized Tish's voice immediately because he'd talked to her on the phone so many times. She'd been Caroline's roommate when Burke and Caroline had first started dating. There was a little animosity between her and him because Tish had been forced to move out so Burke could move in. It really hadn't been that big a deal since Tish had been talking about buying a condo and had found a great place, but Caroline said Tish still felt a little hurt.

"Hey, Tish. How's it going?"

"I'm drunk. You?"

"Pretty much the same."

He heard the sound of glass against glass. "I brought you something."

"What's that?"

"Tequila. I thought we could do a shot together."

Burke laughed. "Kind of hard to do while I'm tied up."

"Just tilt your head back. I'll do the rest." Tish clinked the glasses together again. "Come on. I really want to do a shot with you."

Burke tilted his head back. "Okay."

Tish managed to align the glass with his mouth in the dark. "Okay. Ready. One, two, three."

She tipped the glass and he swallowed, feeling the slow burn of tequila down his throat. It wasn't a perfect shot, though, and some trickled down his chin. "You missed."

"Oops. Sorry. Hard to do this in the dark."

"Tell me about it."

He could feel her breath on his face. She smelled like lime and Cuervo.

"Let me get that for you," she said, right before she kissed him. She tasted like tequila, too.

Burke kissed her back. Partly because he was drunk, partly because he was horny, and partly because it was impossible to resist her soft, warm, wet lips. This was what the game was all about, he reasoned. This was what Caroline wanted to happen.

Tish sucked his bottom lip between hers before slipping her tongue in his mouth. "You taste good," she murmured against his mouth. "It's too bad I'm not allowed to do more. I like to suck."

His cock grew another inch.

He made a strangled sound in his throat because that was all he was capable of at the moment. Which didn't seem to bother Tish, because she kept kissing him. With his head tilted back against the chair and her hand cradling his jaw, she kissed him like she was going to devour him. He felt himself straining against the ties that bound his arms, wanting to pull her down on his lap and rub her against his erection. He couldn't move, though. All he could do was endure Tish's oral assault and hope he didn't come in his pants.

"Time's up," Caroline called from the other side of the door.

Tish didn't stop kissing him and, heaven help him, Burke didn't want her to. Finally, after Caroline knocked again and suggested Tish might want to move her ass *now*, Tish pulled away and ruffled his hair.

"Wow."

They were both breathing hard.

"Yeah, wow," Burke said. "Thanks."

"You're welcome." He could hear her opening the door. "Hey, Burke?"

"Yeah?"

"I still think you're a little bit of an asshole, but you're a great kisser."

The door closed behind her.

Burke only had a moment to get his breathing under control before the door opened again. Tish had him spinning from the tequila and the kissing. He had no idea what to expect next.

"Uh, hi, welcome to my closet." Humor was the only thing that was going to get him through this situation, he decided. "I'd offer you a seat, but I seem to be tied to the only one."

"You're funny, dude."

Burke choked on his own saliva. It was a guy. This one was easy to figure out, too. It was Jeff, a creative director Caroline worked with at the advertising agency where she was a copywriter. Jeff and Caroline shared an office, but Jeff had never struck Burke as a threat before. For one, he was fresh out of college and looked like he was twelve. For another, his hobbies included skateboarding and comic books. Jeff was like the kid brother you couldn't wait to see at Christmas. Now, Burke was recognizing what a threat Jeff really was.

"So," Burke said, "is everyone enjoying torturing me?"

Jeff snorted. "Hell, yeah. Caroline is drunk off her ass and telling us what she's going to do when it's her turn in here. And what did you do to Natalie, dude? She's grinning like the cat that got the canary."

"What can I do? I'm tied up."

"Oh, yeah."

There was a long moment of silence. A bead of sweat trickled underneath Burke's blindfold and along the side of his nose before being absorbed by the cloth.

Burke said, "I don't think I'm drunk enough for this not to be weird."

"I'm drunk enough. I'm just not gay enough."

Burke felt Jeff brush against him and he stiffened. "What are you doing, Jeff?"

"Just moving. I'm a little claustrophobic." He shifted again, bumping into the closet door. "Damn. That was my head."

Burke could hear peals of laughter outside the door. "They think something is going on in here."

Jeff laughed. "They wish."

"Maybe we should let them think there is," Burke said. He might not have been drunk enough for a little man-on-man action, but he was drunk enough to pretend. "What do you think?"

In response, Jeff let out a long, low moan. It made the hair on the back of Burke's neck stand up because it sounded for all the world like a guy in the middle of an orgasm. Not that he had all that much experience with such noises, other than his own, but he'd watched enough porn.

The laughter outside stopped.

Burke wet his lips. If Jeff could do it, he could, too. He moaned. Softly. Then more loudly.

"Oh, God, man," Jeff said, getting into the spirit of things. "Oh, man."

Burke could all but hear the eyes popping on the other side of the door. He panted a little to Jeff's accompanying banging on the closet door. "Yes, oh, yes!"

"Time's up," Caroline called from the other side of the door. "Save some for me."

"You're all right, dude. And braver than I am."

"How so?"

"Benji's going to be champing at the bit to get in here with you now that he thinks you swing both ways."

Burke swallowed hard, a knot of cold dread lodging behind his breastbone. He'd forgotten about Benji. Benji, Caroline's next-door neighbor. Benji, who was an excellent cook and a long-distance runner. He was also very, very gay.

"Oh, fuck."

"Good luck, dude."

The door closed behind Jeff, leaving Burke once again alone for a moment. Surprisingly, even the news that Benji might be molesting him momentarily hadn't dissuaded his erection. His cock throbbed between his legs as if it had a mind of its own. Burke knew from experience that it did, but not enough to want to make an appearance for Benji. He didn't think so, anyway.

The door opened and closed. There were only two people left besides Caroline. Benji and Caroline's Pilates buddy, Martha.

"Hey," he said. "Hope you don't mind sloppy seconds, or is it thirds?"

"Sounds like you and Jeff had a good time. I didn't know you went that way."

Burke let out a breath he hadn't realized he was holding. It was Martha. Of course, that meant Benji was coming up next, but Burke put that thought out of his mind.

"We were just messing around," he said. "Giving you girls a show."

"Oh."

Silence. Burke shifted. It wasn't just his cock that was starting to stiffen up. "So. How's things?"

"Burke?" Martha asked, her voice low and soft. "Can I tell you something?"

"Sure, Martha."

"I have wanted to fuck you since I met you." She giggled. "That's a relief."

"You're pretty drunk, aren't you?"

Martha didn't say anything. He felt her brush against his knees and realized she had moved around to the front of him. The closet was a walk-in, and all the coats were now piled on the couch in the living room, but it was still a tight fit for two bodies and a chair, especially when one of those bodies was very well endowed.

Martha was short enough that her breasts brushed against his face as she straddled his bound legs. She smelled nice—a sweet, floral scent—and she felt good against him, too. She wasn't sitting on his lap, just leaning against him with her hands resting on his shoulders.

"I can't fuck you," she said, sounding sad. "But I thought we could play a little bit."

"Okay."

She sat on his lap then, turning sideways because the arms of the chair wouldn't accommodate her straddling him face to face, and her bottom brushed his erection. "Wow. You're huge. I thought Caroline was just exaggerating."

Burke laughed uncomfortably. "Thanks."

She shifted around on his lap, and he wasn't quite sure what she was doing until she leaned forward and pressed her bare breasts to his face. "I've seen you staring at them," she whispered.

"I'm sorry," Burke said, finding it hard to concentrate with so much warm, soft flesh in his face. "You're very pretty."

"I'm chubby, but I've got a nice rack."

Burke wasn't one to argue with a lady. He nuzzled his face against her breasts, his cock throbbing.

"Mmm, that's nice," she breathed against the top of his head. "Would you suck my nipples? That'll get me off."

Burke had only to turn his head to the side to capture one hard nipple between his lips. He sucked it into his mouth, her skin tasting as sweet as she smelled. She whimpered and shifted on his lap. He sucked harder, the steady, slurping sound filling the closet.

He turned his head to take the other nipple in his mouth, and her hand was there, holding her breast and feeding it to him. He ran his teeth lightly over her skin, sucking and wetting it until she was slippery against him.

"Oh, oh, yes," she moaned. "Just like that. Suck it."

He obliged, pausing only long enough to switch to the opposite nipple, sucking rhythmically until she squirmed on his lap and started to come with a gasp. She pressed her ample breasts against his face, all but smothering him as she writhed on his lap. "Oh, Burke!"

He let her nipple slip from between his lips only when he was sure she had finished. It was a first for him, getting a woman off like that, and he was so hard it hurt.

The sharp knocking at the door startled Martha and she quickly shifted off his lap. "Oh, God," she said breathlessly. "Thank you, thank you."

"Just make sure you're all buttoned up," Burke said, ignoring the ringing in his ears and the way his head was spinning. "They don't need to know what was going on."

Martha took a deep breath. "Right. Okay. Thanks, Burke. That was fun."

The door opened and closed before Burke could respond.

His heart was hammering in his chest. The thought that Benji would be the next to share his closet space did nothing to deter his erection. He'd been hard for so long he ached. He needed release and he needed it soon.

The door opened again. He took a breath. It wouldn't be so bad. Benji wouldn't do anything he didn't agree to. The problem, of course, was that he was afraid of what he might agree to with his cock bursting through the front of his pants. The door closed. It was the moment of truth.

"Hey," he said, trying not to sound the way he felt. Which was horny, drunk, nervous, freaked out—and horny. "How's it going, man?"

A hand ran through his hair, settling on the back of his neck. He flinched, but there was nowhere for him to go.

"So what have you guys been doing out there?" Even to his own ears he sounded a little strained. "I feel like I've been in here forever."

Warm, wet lips silenced him. Warm, wet, *familiar* lips.

"Caroline?" he asked, pulling back as far as his restraints and the chair would allow him, which wasn't much. "Is that you?"

She pulled off his blindfold, and there was just enough light coming under the door for him to make out her smiling face. "Who'd you think it was, Benji?"

"Well, yeah."

She kissed him again, harder this time. "Not disappointed, are you?"

"Oh, babe, you have no idea how relieved I am."

Caroline tugged his shirt free and unbuckled his belt. "Good, because after that little scene with Jeff, I was starting to wonder. I'm happy to see you're still dressed."

He laughed. "Where's Benji?"

"He had to leave about ten minutes ago. He said to tell you he was very disappointed he didn't get his turn and that you owe him." She unzipped his pants and slipped her hand inside. "I told him that after tonight you'd probably need at least a week's rest."

Burke groaned when she squeezed his cock. "At least a week."

"Oh, baby. You're so fucking hard." She pulled away and he heard the sound of rustling cloth. "I've been dying to get in here. Seven minutes is a long time when there are four other people ahead of you."

"This was your idea," Burke reminded her. "Maybe next time you'll think—"

He lost his voice when he felt her wet, wet pussy slide against his cock. She was facing away from him, the only way they could possibly have sex, with the chair arms getting in the way of her straddling more than his knees. But this way, with her facing the door and her ass in his lap, he could slide inside her. Except she wasn't guiding him inside her wetness, she was only teasing him by rubbing up and down the length of his aching erection.

"You feel so good," she sighed. "I can't wait to have you inside me."

Burke shifted in the chair, slouching down, trying to find the warm wetness she was keeping from him. "Come here, baby," he begged. "Let me inside you. Let me fuck you."

She wiggled against him. "Yeah? You want to fuck me? Don't you want to tell me what you've been doing in here with my friends?"

"Later. I need to be inside you."

She shifted slightly and slid back against him, taking the full, hard length of him inside her pussy. Nothing had ever felt so good to him in his life. She slid forward, until just the head of his cock was nestled between her plump lips, before sliding back again and taking him deep inside.

"Fuck me," he said through gritted teeth. "Fuck me, Caroline."

She obeyed, riding his cock hard, slamming down on his lap until the chair creaked under the weight of them. He knew it wouldn't take him long to come, he'd been ready to explode since she'd unzipped his pants, but she came first, her pussy rippling around his cock as she whimpered and moaned.

Even though she'd slowed her motions and was only rocking on him now, enjoying her orgasm, the feeling of her pussy tight around his cock was enough to send him over the edge. He bucked up against her, feeling his orgasm building deep down in his gut and exploding up out of his cock. Over and over he thrust into her as much as his restraints would allow as she undulated against him, milking him, driving him out of his mind.

Finally, he was finished. It felt like the longest orgasm of his life. "Wow, babe. That was incredible."

"I'm glad," she said, sounding breathless. "Because our time's up."

He groaned. "Do we really have to go back out there? They're going to know what we were doing in here, and I really don't feel like enduring any more cracks."

"They're gone," Caroline said, working at the ties on his wrists. "I sent them all home when Martha came out looking like a guilty teenager with her blouse buttoned all wrong."

Burke could feel the heat in his cheeks, but felt no need to explain now. Right now, all he wanted was to get out of the damned closet and get naked with his girlfriend. "If you sent them home, why didn't you just let me out of here so we could do this right?"

Caroline giggled with wicked promise. "Because, silly boy, I wanted my seven minutes in heaven."

EMERALD

WHO'S ON TOP?

"GOT A GAME in your head?"

These were the first words Corey ever said to me, startling me as he approached unseen from behind. I was standing in my neighborhood park, gazing at the silent baseball field in front of me. It's a simple field, situated in the far corner of the park off the soccer field. It doesn't have dugouts or bleachers, just a single metal bench for each team and a chain-link fence that borders the home-plate corner. But a baseball field's a baseball field as far as I'm concerned.

A Yankees fan from birth, I grew up in New York with baseball in my blood; my parents met each other at Yankee Stadium during game six of the 1977 World Series. Having moved away from home but stayed on the East Coast, I still go home for a game several times a summer. But for the most part I have to make do now catching them on TV every chance I get.

In the meantime, I like to visit this field whenever I find myself at the park. My favorite time to come is at dusk, when the no-use-after-dark rule of the park is just about to take effect and parents are starting to gather their little ones and hurry home. I sit on the benches, wander the baselines, lean against the chain-link fence behind home plate, appreciating whatever it is that attracts me about an empty playing field at night.

It was there I stood that evening mid-season, fingers laced through the metal as I watched the sun setting on the horizon behind second base, when I heard those words: *Got a game in your head?*

Turning, I saw an intriguingly hot stranger walking toward me, hands in his jeans pockets. He smiled as he put his hand out.

"Sorry, I didn't mean to startle you. My name's Corey."

"Paige," I said, stepping away from the fence and reaching to shake his hand. Glancing back at the field, I smiled and said, "I was just having a solitary moment of baseball appreciation."

Corey laughed. "Yeah, I know what you mean."

And he did, I could tell. I gazed into his striking dark brown eyes and felt the heat of arousal stirring in me. He joined me at the fence, and we turned back toward the field as darkness fell.

We exchanged numbers, but as it turned out neither of us had a chance to call before we ran into each other the next day in the exact same place. I didn't usually find myself at the park so early in the afternoon, but I had decided to watch the coed community youth baseball league game, and as I strolled up to the field, I caught sight of him, arms crossed as he leaned against the fence behind the benches of one of the teams. Surprised by the coincidence, I started toward him. Before I reached him, he turned his head. Immediately I noticed the red *B* on his hat and I stopped.

He was a Red Sox fan.

I narrowed my eyes at him with half-serious malevolence. He hadn't seen me yet. At that moment, he turned my way, and his face lit up when his eyes met mine. Then they dropped slightly to my jacket.

I was wearing my Yankees pullover, and his expression immediately shifted to one of surprise—and then to a challenging gaze similar to mine. We were both aware, I was sure, that our respective teams would be facing off that very night with the first of a three-game series against each other in New York. Still standing a good twenty yards away from him, I lifted my head and looked him up and down. Then I stared hard at him, holding back a smile. Even as I felt the heat rising in me, I tossed my head and turned on my heel. I felt him watching my ass as I walked haughtily back in the direction from which I had come.

A *Red Sox* fan. Unbelievable.

My team had better win tonight, I told myself.

The phone rang as I was pulling the half-gallon container of chocolate-chip-cookie-dough ice cream from the freezer.

"Gearing up to watch your team get its ass kicked, I imagine," Corey said.

A shot of arousal coursed through me. I frowned slightly and tried to quash it. Now was not the time to get friendly with a Red Sox fan. Still, I smiled as I said, "Actually, I'm getting ready to watch my Yankees pound their perpetually inferior rivals. Is there something I can do for you?"

"I was thinking maybe we could watch the game together."

"It's not going to bother you to have a gloating Yankee diehard rubbing your loss in your face for nine innings?"

"As long as you're okay with the other way around when the inevitable happens," he countered.

Rising irresistibly to his challenge, I said immediately, "You're on."

The bell rang just as the national anthem was coming to a close. I marched to the door and opened it to find him standing on the threshold, cap on his head and a cocky, challenging expression on his face.

With a similar expression on my face, I stepped back to let him in. He smiled and stepped closer, kissing me without pretense. Forgetting everything but my horniness for a moment, I kissed him back as his hand snaked around my waist and down to my ass.

Breathless, we broke apart and laughed. "So," I said. "You're a Sox fan."

"All my life," he grinned and moved past me as I shut the door.

I gestured toward the couch and followed him to it. "Can I get you anything?"

His eyes flicked quickly up and down me. "No, thanks," he answered as he settled on the couch. I sat down beside him. He turned to me. "I've never had sex with a Yankee fan before," he remarked.

I raised my eyebrows at him. "Should I take that as an indication that you believe we're going to have sex?"

He laughed. "Something about the look you managed to give me even in your disgust made me think it was on your mind."

— 54 —

I smirked. "Aren't you perceptive? I was planning to fuck you from the second I met you. I just didn't plan on your being one of 'them.'"

Turning to the TV screen, I took in the scene of the stadium where I'd seen the same match-up in person many times. Instantly, I felt the familiar energy of my disdain for the opposing team. Out of the corner of my eye, I could see the same tension enveloping Corey.

He turned to me again. "Interested in making a little bet on this game?"

"What kind of bet?"

He leaned in a little closer. "Winner gets to have his—or her—way with the loser, so to speak."

I looked at him. "Excuse me?"

"Winner gets to dominate," he explained.

I blinked. After an instant of surprise, I smiled as I realized immediately what a twist that would present for me. I wondered briefly if any of the same conflict was stirring in him as I glanced down at his hand, extended toward me to shake on the deal. After a moment I slipped mine into it. We grasped firmly, our gazes hardened.

Born and raised in New York, I come from a family of unswerving, die-hard Yankee fans; I'd lived and breathed the Yankees ever since I was old enough to know what they were. It went without saying that I wanted my team to win. Always. And *especially* when they were playing the Red Sox.

But I also love to be dominated.

Two nights later, I carried the bottle of red wine to the coffee table and set the glasses on coasters. A knock on the door came as I headed back to the kitchen. I stopped to open it, and Corey entered with a grin, kissing me as he shut the door behind him. I returned his smile and flipped off the kitchen light as we went by.

As we made our way to the sofa, both of us affected a casual countenance, pretending to ignore the fact that this was the night of nights for our little game. I had to admit that it was throwing my lifelong team loyalty into turmoil, subverting it for the first time in my life—this simple desire to be thrown/pushed/held/tied down and fucked hard, no less.

Tonight was the third and final game of this Yankees/Red Sox series. I had been relegated—by my own agreement in shaking on the bet—to being Corey's sex slave for the hour after the first game ended two nights before, and even now I grew wet as I recalled his pushing me to my knees and grabbing the back of my head as he shoved his cock down my throat. Last night had brought a switch in my favor (as far as baseball was concerned, anyway). My boys had pummeled the Red Sox 9 to 1, and Corey had been forced to sit back to receive some of his own. While he dominated beautifully, I had no question that he got off on submission, too. I'd seen his cock grow hard as I shoved him facedown over the back of the couch and smacked his ass until it was bright red, holding his face against the cushions by the back of his neck.

"Here you go," Corey said as he finished pouring and handed me my wineglass, snapping me back to the present. I took a deep breath, still wet from my thoughts. In my head, I knew I wanted the Yankees to win tonight—as always. An uncontrollable intensity in my body, however, pulled insistently with the desire to be dominated—held down and fucked hard in utter submission.

I tried to sit still on the couch, but the unpredictable nature of our little game was becoming almost unbearably frustrating to me. I just wanted to fuck. Corey sat down beside me, and I knew I wasn't going to last the whole game. The Red Sox were up; as their batter slid safely into second, Corey turned to me with that gleam in his eye and grabbed my hair, pulling me in for a hard kiss.

"Are you trying to suggest we go play by play tonight?" I asked a little breathlessly as he broke the kiss.

"Maybe inning by inning." He grinned.

I couldn't remember another game when I'd looked forward to the commercial breaks.

"Walk this way," Corey said as he grabbed his keys and headed toward the door.

"Where are we going?" I couldn't resist asking, surprised. The Red Sox victory was his cue to lead me to whichever room he chose and do what he would with me. The thought made me shiver even as I cast one last glare at the final score before pressing the POWER button on the remote.

Apparently, he wasn't choosing a room this time. "That's for me to know," he said as we headed outside. He opened his passenger door for me, and we drove in silence. A slow smile spread across my face in the dark as he pulled up along the curb by the park where we'd met. He avoided the lot so as not to arouse suspicion, since the park was closed after dark. Having been in this park at night many times, I was aware that the cops usually came and did an obligatory drive-through about one a.m. and only checked it that once. I certainly hoped tonight wouldn't be an exception.

I followed him through the darkness, our feet rustling the lush grass. That was the only sound; it was so quiet I could hear my breathing. As we approached the chain-link fence where we'd met, he cut around past the dugout bench and walked onto the field. He led me by home plate and stopped at the fence directly behind it.

Dropping on the ground a small bag I had seen him grab from his backseat, he reached for my waist and pulled me into position in front of the fence. Crushing me against it, he kissed me hard before backing up slightly and pushing me onto my knees by my shoulders.

"Don't move," he ordered as he reached for the bag. He pulled a rope of some sort out of it and moved behind me. I felt my wrists being grabbed and tied together behind my back.

Moving in front of me once more, he freed his cock with one hand and grabbed a fistful of my hair with the other. The smell of the freshly mown field wafted around us, and I breathed it in heavily as I looked up at him, stars slathered across the black background above him. He ran a finger along my jawline, slowly, gently, as I shifted from knee to knee on the sandy gravel. It dug into my skin, but my arousal was too overt for me to care. I was wet and fidgety as he held my head away from him, my mouth almost watering for the taste of his cock.

He slipped his finger lightly into my mouth, still holding my hair solidly to keep me from diving forward onto his cock like I wanted to. I looked up at him again, and when I met his eyes, I knew suddenly that he understood exactly what effect this was having on me. He pulled his hand back away from me and positioned it on his cock. Slowly, he stroked himself, holding my head back and not letting me move. I had never wanted a cock in my mouth so badly. Finally, Corey

— 58 —

reached under my chin and turned my face roughly upward, making me meet his eyes.

"You ready to suck this cock?"

"Yes, please," I said. He looked at me for another moment before grabbing another fistful of my hair with his free hand and shoving my face forward, pushing his cock deep into my throat. I almost gagged, but I had anticipated enough that I had time to breathe correctly. It was fortunate that I knew a thing or two about giving head—even by pseudo force.

He held my head in position for a few seconds before letting off and then pushing it rhythmically. The gravel was still biting into my knees, the ropes binding my wrists chafing slightly as I shifted my hands. Corey's hard length penetrated my lips repeatedly, banging against the back of my throat as my pussy got wetter by the second. Finally, he yanked my hair back and pulled my head off his cock. I looked up at him, his eyes like solid dark chocolate as he lifted me to my feet.

Reaching behind me, he untied the rope holding my wrists and pushed me back up against the fence before reaching for the bag again. He pulled out two more ropes, identical to the first.

"Spread your legs."

I did so, and he proceeded to tie each of my ankles to the fence. When he was done, he stood and attended to my wrists, lifting them over my head and binding them to the chainlink as well. When he stepped back, I was firmly bound, standing, by all four limbs to the fence behind home plate.

Corey hitched my denim skirt up to my waist. I had nothing on underneath, and I was sure he could see how wet I was just by looking, and he did seem pleased when he stared between my legs.

"You like what I'm doing to you, baby?" he taunted, brushing his fingers between my legs. I gasped and couldn't keep from crying out just a little. Immediately I bit my lip and gave him a look of apology.

"I didn't think I'd have to tell you to be quiet here, Paige. Are you going to be a good girl, or do you need a gag?"

I shook my head. "No. I'll be good."

"You'd better."

Corey leaned in and ran his tongue across my lips, pulling back slightly whenever I tried to meet his mouth and kiss him. I squirmed in frustration.

Abruptly I felt his finger enter me; I hadn't known it was anywhere near me. I shrieked quietly, wincing as I realized I'd just broken the rules.

"Mmm-hmm," Corey said shortly, backing off and returning to the bag. "I see you're having some trouble following the rules tonight." He wasn't smiling as he pulled a ball gag from the bag.

"I didn't mean to. I won't do it again," I pleaded as he advanced toward me with the gag. I submitted sorrowfully as he installed it in my mouth.

Quickly, he pulled open the snaps on my shirt, then popped the front clasp on my bra. The warm night breeze graced my breasts while he watched my nipples get hard. I shivered. Then he grabbed them roughly, pushing his body up against mine and kissing me. My pussy went into overdrive and begged for release as he squeezed my tits in his fists.

He pulled back and fumbled with his cock, putting on a condom. I breathed heavily, my tits exposed to the night, my skirt at my waist, my wrists bound above me and ropes around my ankles holding my legs spread wide. Corey advanced back toward me and reached up to grasp my throat solidly, pushing my head back against the hard, chain-link fence. I felt the wetness between my legs start to drip.

With a grunt, he pushed into me, still gripping his choke hold on me, his other hand now laced through the chain-link fence near my head. He pumped me hard, eventually grasping my hips with both hands for better traction as I moaned as much as I could through the gag. It was good that it was there, it occurred to me, so my screams weren't heard by the quiet neighborhood households nearby.

When he finished, Corey pulled out and looked me up and down. He stood back, removing the condom and zipping up his jeans. Moving forward, he reached to remove the gag from my mouth.

"I want to hear you call my name in my ear when you come," he stated. "But not too loud—we don't want to wake up any of the nice suburban neighbors." With that, he reached for my clit and gently ran his finger across it.

Urgency took my breath away. I pulled at the restraints on my wrists, desperately wanting to touch myself along with him. He noticed and smiled.

"Sorry, doll, this is my game now, remember? You lost tonight. Your hands will stay where I put them until I say so."

His voice and his words, taunting me, made me squirm under his ever rougher touch, needing release. It was building, and there was nothing left for me to do but give in, relinquish all control inside myself; outside I already had none.

"Come for me—now. Now, Paige." Corey's voice got rough, and I screamed full force as my body exploded, Corey's hand moving immediately to cover my mouth and muffle the sound. The restraints holding my limbs suddenly served to protect me from gravity as every nerve in my body let go and flowed instantaneously with the orgasm that consumed it. Behind me, the fence jangled and swished, the reverberation rippling to the top of the chain-link fence twenty feet up like an extension of the orgasmic waves ripping through my body. When it was over, I hung limply, trying to catch my breath and emitting tiny breathless sobs forced out of me by pure intensity.

Corey smiled and moved in to kiss me, softly this time, as he reached up to untie my wrists. When that was done, he attended carefully to my ankles, dropping the restraints one by one back into the little bag he'd brought with him. Then he pulled me gently to him, his arms around my waist.

Still a little out of breath, I set my head against his shoulder for a moment and took a deep breath. Then I let go and stepped back, returning his smile as he retrieved the bag from the ground. A breathless little laugh escaped me as I turned toward the street.

We walked without speaking back through the grass to his car, Corey placing his hand lightly on the small of my back as we crossed up a hill, as if we were a couple walking together to the valet after dinner in a lovely restaurant instead of two people who barely knew each other who had just engaged in bondage sex in a park after hours.

Back at my house, he left his bag in the car as we entered through the front door. I retrieved my own carefully packed bag that I had set out in anticipation and returned it to the closet. Corey noticed.

"And what's that?" he asked, seeming genuinely surprised.

"You think you're the only one who knows the art of preparation?" I asked him. Closing the closet door, I pictured the brand-new strap-on dildo tucked away in the bottom of my bag and reminded him, "Don't forget, Corey dear, we've still got half a season left. You may have gotten lucky tonight—but I think we both know who's going to come out on top."

PLAYING FOR KEEPS

G REG'S SITTING AT A TABLE in the bar when I walk in. I've been waiting for this moment for what feels like forever. He's coolly sipping his pint, but his eyes have the same evil glint as mine do. Of course, we're meeting as friends. But we both know that we'll be leaving as lovers. We just haven't told each other yet.

"Evening," he says.

"Evening. That mine?" I gesture at the second pint on the table.

"Well, I'm not meeting anyone else."

"Makes a change," I say, teasing.

He smiles. We have an ongoing joke that he's a slut.

He is.

But so am I.

I sit, feeling my suspenders dig into me, my silk knickers getting damp. Stockings aren't my usual choice, so I still notice when I wear them, but I like the way my lingerie looks—and feels—on me. I'm in control when I get dressed up. The entire seduction process arouses me, from start to finish. I've been wet since I started getting ready for him, planning what I was going to do, choosing the silk lingerie, the ideal subtle outfit to hide it. After all, I don't want to accidentally flash my stocking tops. I don't want him to see what he's getting until I'm good and ready. I don't want him to be sure. Not yet. He'll realize eventually, when he sees what I'm wearing underneath my clothes. But he's going to have to work for that.

I sit opposite him, legs stretched out, not brushing against him but close enough for him to feel my presence. We chat, small talk at first but soon progressing to our usual joking, teasing, and eventually, flirting.

At every point that things look like they could go further, one or the other of us makes an excuse to break off conversation; another round, a trip to the loo, or a visit to the fag machine. We're both enjoying the power game, unsure as to who'll crack first. It's like playing chicken, but rather than seeing who'll veer away first, we're seeing who'll take that final step over the mark.

And we're both playing to win.

I enjoy looking at him—following the contours of his face with my eyes, trying to identify exactly what it is that attracts me to him. The eyes, still glinting with promise—whether he intends to keep it or not? The bone structure—traditional, strong, classically appealing? The lips? Not full but not thin; I can tell to look at them that they'll feel good against mine. As I said, I'm a slut. I can just tell.

Maybe it's his body. It's certainly toned enough, and I know from hugging him good night that it fits well into mine.

But no, as he makes some dry comment and lust shoots through me, I know it's got more to do with his mind than the way he looks. The packaging is just an added bonus.

I smile, make some crack of my own back, and there's another eye meet. I hold his gaze longer than strictly proper, lick my lips, just slightly, nothing porn star about it, then carefully push my tight skirt up under the table to just above my stockings. I checked earlier in the mirror: I know there's a slight time lag when I stand up, when my stocking tops show. I also know it looks accidental.

"Another pint?"

"Sure." He seems glad that the moment is broken. I stand up to go to the bar, struggling not to look back to see if he saw my flash—and if he did, what his response was.

When I return, I sit almost imperceptibly closer, near enough for me to feel the heat of his body against my leg but still not quite touching. I can hear my heart in my head, feel it in my clit with every pulse, but still we talk. I notice him shift in his chair as I make some particularly provocative comment, and hope it's because I'm making him uncomfortable.

He stands to go to the loo and I see his jeans are bulging. I feel proud. Until I realize the bastard is playing me at my own game. My cunt is flooding and I'm mentally picturing his cock. Is he cut or uncut? How big is he? What does it taste like? He's returning the flash. And it's working.

He doesn't look back, either.

I can feel my arousal rising. My pelvis is warm, tingles going from clit to chest, nipples stiffening beneath my T-shirt, clearly visible. Which will show him he's winning when he gets back—but, I realize, will also help me reassert control. Because men are easy like that. Rather than batting away the thoughts of his cock, I dwell on them, imagining taking him into my mouth, feeling his cock stiffen further, tasting his salty pre-come and breathing in his scent as I slide my lips millimeter by millimeter down his shaft, not moving at any point until I hear him groan.

It has the desired effect.

I'm lost in my headfuck when he returns, and I catch him shooting a glance at my nipples.

One–love to me.

He leans over. I think he's caved as his hand slides toward my neck. He touches me. Softly. Raising the fine hairs on the back of my neck. I can't suppress my shudder. Then, "Ow!"

I see him holding a fine gray hair between his fingers.

"Thought you'd want this pulled out."

Love–all.

His eyes are dancing now. I know he felt my response. I need to score some points back. And quickly.

I start chatting; nonflirtatious—something to do with work. As I talk, I gradually lean forward, by a process of animated hand gestures. I know he can see down my top. I chose it because it gapes at the front. I love cowl necks. I remember the feeling of his hand on my neck, controlling the delicious shiver at the memory but ensuring that my nipples stay stiff. And then, the gamble. I make sure I'm drinking quickly so I constantly have a mouthful of beer. At the next joke he makes, I laugh harder than normal, beer spurting from my mouth. Only a small amount, but still not a good look. But it does mean that beer is drizzling down my neck, heading toward my breasts, which he—and no one else in the bar—can see.

He shifts again, as I feel the drop trail down my collarbone, between my breasts, one trickle sliding toward my nipple.

He's still talking but then he stumbles across his words; something he never normally does.

One–love.

I want the game to move on.

"Shit."

I put my hand on my collarbone, leaning back, and wipe my breast clean of beer. He can't see me stroking my breast close up. But he can clearly see the outline of my hand under my top. I rub myself clean then bring my hand to my mouth and lick my finger clean. Again, more perfunctory than porn star, but I take rather longer about it than I otherwise would, glancing down "Princess Di style" as I do. After all, I'm not flirting. I'm simply sucking beer from my fingers.

"Shame to waste it."

He doesn't reply. I look up.

"Bitch." His tone is light, but he's slipped. He's given a response. *Thirty–love.*

"What?"

"Nothing."

He realizes he's losing. The clock is ticking. The pub is only open for another thirty minutes. And I need him to invite me back.

"Did I tell you about Ella?"

Oooh, he's playing dirty. The "see if I can make her jealous" ruse. I get a flicker of indignation but push it back.

"No. Go on."

"Met her at a party last week. One of those instant lust things. God, could she suck cock. Might have to see her again."

He's playing really dirty. He knows I consider blow jobs "my territory." My gut instinct is to brag about my own abilities, but no. I hold back.

"Men and blow jobs. You're so easy. And you all think you know how to give head." I laugh.

The ball is in his court.

"Some of us do," he says.

Forty–love.

"And I'm going to have you coming in my face by the end of tonight."

Game.

I do like to win.

BONNIE DEE

SHOWTIME

GAMES BRING A LITTLE EXCITEMENT and joy into our humdrum lives. Everybody wants to play at being a little nasty. Nobody wants to get caught.

Well, maybe they do, a little.

I used to play a game that let me walk on the wild side without actually doing anything *too* wild. Although in my late twenties, when I put on my old high school uniform and pulled my hair into pigtails, I still looked enticingly illegal. I wore that classic pleated skirt with no panties underneath, slipped my patent-leather shoes on over white bobby socks, buttoned my white Oxford shirt over my braless breasts, and strolled down to the Blue Heron Theater, where the triple-X movies were shown.

On the few short blocks from my apartment to the theater, the constant breeze in the Windy City threatened to lift my skirt like Marilyn Monroe's. I struggled to keep the plaid pleats in place. Okay, sometimes I didn't try very hard, giving passersby a glimpse of rounded ass or smoothly waxed pussy beneath the skirt.

Paying for my ticket at the dingy box office, I slowly counted out dollar bills, allowing the ticket seller a long look at my barely covered cleavage. Since only one or two buttons of the shirt were fastened, there was plenty of skin for him to admire.

The ticket guy was young, probably a college student who was happy to have a job that gave him plenty of time to study in between selling tickets and manning the concession counter. His floppy brown hair straggled down over his eyes. As he sold me my ticket, he shook his head and half smiled.

I smiled back, took my ticket and twitched my ass as I walked from the lobby into the darkened theater.

These days, most guys prefer their porn in the privacy of their homes on their computers or TV, but at the time, there were still a few die-hard theater devotees getting their rocks off watching *Barely Legal XVIII: Fuck Me Tender, Fuck Me Sweet.* When I sashayed into the run-down theater looking like a fresh-faced, sex-bomb teenager, all eyes locked on me instead of the screen. But just to make sure I had their attention, I made my presence known, sometimes pretending to drop change and bending over to pick up imaginary coins from the floor. I flashed the fellows an ass they'd never see the likes of outside of electronic images or strip clubs. I was their fantasy come true and I was glad to provide that service. Made me feel kind of like Florence Nightingale tending the wounded.

I scanned the theater for a likely subject, then sat only a few chairs away from my mark, perhaps a middle-aged man in a baseball cap.

Catching his gaping gaze, I nodded and smiled, then turned my attention to the movie. For his benefit, I stared wide-eyed and shocked as if my virginal eyes had never seen anything like it before.

If the guy's gaze wandered to the movie, I let out a little gasp to bring his attention back to me. "Oh, my God, I can't believe this!" I murmured low, a hand covering my mouth. I giggled and cast a sideways glance at my mark.

When I was sure he was watching, I began my private show. I squirmed in my seat, making the sexy schoolgirl skirt ride higher and higher on my thighs. "Ooh! That's disgusting," I repeated my expression of shock over the action on the screen, but my legs pressed tight together, squeezing my clit. Reaching down, I casually pulled the skirt up until my naked pussy was revealed.

I whimpered, moaned, and squirmed some more and it was hardly an act. My pussy was hard and aching with need by the time my hand reached it. I traced a finger along the hot, wet seam in between the folds of my labia then drew the juices up onto my clit. I tickled it in little circles, gasping at the sensation and half closing my eyes.

A quick glance confirmed my audience of one was still engrossed.

I let my legs fall wide open, allowing him an up-close-and-personal view. After diddling my clit for a while, I slid my hand back down between my thighs and plunged several fingers into my hole. It was slick, the muscles clenching tight around my probing fingers. I moaned a little louder with each thrust.

My silent partner had his cock out, stroking briskly up and down in time with my finger fucking. He gave a choked groan as our mutual rhythm sped up.

I gasped and writhed in my theater seat. Juices trickled down my thighs, wetting the rough, worn upholstery beneath me. My fingers didn't measure up to a good, thick cock, even when I drove four of them in and out of my cunt. Soon I had as much of my hand as I could fit thrusting into me. The naughtiness of my erotic show enhanced my slowly building orgasm. Sparkles of delight gathered from the dark reaches of my body to coalesce in my sex.

Another glance at my partner in crime verified he was ready to come, too. His hand slid up and down his cock with dogged persistence. If I was truly Florence Nightingale I'd have been down there with my face in his lap, giving head, but mutual masturbation was all I cared to share with this stranger.

I was scarcely aware of my audience now, but if I looked around I knew I'd see necks craning as other patrons of the Blue Heron tried to view what was going on in row twelve, seat three. I applied the finger of my other hand to my clit, giving the last bit of stimulation I needed to put me over the edge. I cried out and bucked into my hand sharply several times, then collapsed back in my seat, letting my hand fall slack from between my legs.

A muffled cry to my left alerted me that my seatmate had reached orgasm, too. He jerked and twitched in his chair. I looked with interest at the pale jet of come spilling onto his hand in the dark theater. He panted heavily for several moments. After he'd caught his breath, he opened his eyes to look at me.

I lifted my hand from my lap and licked my fingers as carefully as a cat cleaning its paw. Smoothing my skirt back down over my crotch, I faced him with a sweet smile. "Have a nice day." I rose and walked from the theater, skipping the rest of the movie now that my private show was finished.

With a few subtle variations, this was my game.

But one evening when I walked out of the theater after I'd done my public service, I found the ticket seller sweeping up the lobby. I'd rarely seen him outside his booth, and I was surprised to see that he was pretty hot, with a lean build and sultry, dark eyes. Leaning on his broom, he stared at me, his bedroom eyes reawakening the sparks of desire I'd just laid to rest.

"Finished your business?"

"I'm not a whore," I snapped. "I just like to play."

"You like to play?" He shook the hair back from his eyes and gave me a long, slow once-over that burned my skin like a fever. His eyes locked on mine. A whisper of a smile curved his lips as he reached down and brushed a hand over his crotch. "How'd you like to play with this?"

The game turned on a dime. The young ticket guy was hot and I was still horny. Putting on my sex show for the patrons didn't seem like enough anymore. I craved another level of danger.

I sucked my lower lip into my mouth, then let it go. I scanned his body as he had mine, trying to make him squirm, then nodded my head once. "Okay."

A flicker of surprise shot across his dark eyes. Maybe he thought we were going to stop at flirting. He should have known better. Covering his momentary shock, he reached for the zipper of his fly.

"No." I slunk toward him with a hip-swaying gait. "Not yet. You go down on me first, *then* I'll blow you."

He shrugged. "Whichever."

I liked his compliant attitude. It earned him my smile.

"Let's see what you got." With more force than finesse, he pushed me up against the wall and ripped my shirt open. My breasts bobbed free, heavy yet firm and round. He bent his head to suck my nipple into his mouth. A sharp, pleasurable pain shot like a bolt of electricity from my breast down to my crotch, and I gasped at the unexpected speed of his attack.

He licked and nibbled one rosy bud, then the other, his hand lightly squeezing the breast he wasn't sucking on.

I moaned and arched my chest toward him.

"Oh, baby," he murmured, fondling my tit. "You like that, huh?" He alternated nipping and sucking, twisting and pinching until the powerful surge of neural signals to my crotch almost gave me orgasm number two for the evening.

"Yesss," I hissed. "Now go down on me!"

I liked the ticket seller for obediently dropping to his knees. He pushed up my skirt and covered my smooth cunt with his hot, wet mouth. He gripped my hips in his hands and sucked and licked at my clit.

I thrust my pelvis toward his marvelous mouth and talented tongue. My second orgasm of the evening swelled inside me, much bigger and deeper than the one I'd achieved with my own hand. It burst like fireworks against the dark screen of my closed eyelids. Panting for breath, I collapsed back against the wall. Only the kneeling man's hands kept me upright on my unsteady legs. After a few deep breaths and several trembling aftershocks, I opened my eyes. They flickered and focused, then opened wide with shock.

We had an audience.

Roused by my loud moans and cries, several of the movie patrons had come out to watch the live sex show in the lobby. I would have felt embarrassed if I wasn't so high on sex that I didn't have an ounce of modesty left in me.

Watching the men as they watched me, I knelt down in front of the ticket guy. I pushed his pants down his hips, releasing his cock. It pulsed in my hand, the veins throbbing and the engorged head purple with blood. I continued to gaze at my audience as I placed the head of his cock between my pink-painted lips and sucked it into my mouth. With exaggerated moans of pleasure, I swallowed him deep, then released his glistening length, only to draw it back in again.

Grabbing his ass with both hands to hold him steady, I bobbed my head up and down. My watchers were hauling their cocks out of their pants and stroking in time with me. It was like I was blowing them all at once, and the feeling was powerful. I enjoyed both being on display and the control I had over the men.

The ticket-taker began to groan and buck. He held my head between his hands and pumped into my willing mouth. Suddenly, I wanted him inside me. I stopped sucking and looked up. "Fuck me now!" I ordered.

Give him credit. The boy didn't hesitate or look surprised. He even had the sense to whip a condom from his pocket, which made me wonder if he hadn't sort of planned this. I mean, who bothers to sweep up a XXX-theater lobby?

He pulled me to my feet and pushed me up against the smeary candy counter. Over his shoulder, I continued to gaze at the men while the ticket guy rammed his cock into me. I was wet enough that he slid in easily, but he was big enough that the fit was tight. My inner muscles clenched around him.

"Fuck me. Fuck me hard." I shouted porn-movie dialogue as I clung to him.

He pumped in and out, driving me back against the counter. I wondered if my ass would break the glass before we were finished.

The ticket guy's face was contorted in ecstasy, as were those of a number of the art house patrons lounging against the wall, watching us. Like champagne corks popping, they began to come, one by one.

Turning my attention to my immediate partner, I dug my nails into his back and held on as he shuddered against me. He gave a long, protracted groan as he came. I felt his cock pulse inside me with his releases before he collapsed against me. Luckily, the counter glass held.

By the time we disentangled ourselves, the movie patrons had dispersed either back into the movie theater or out into the street. It was a banner night at the Blue Heron.

As the ticket guy pulled away from me, I lowered my skirt over my dripping pussy and stooped to pick my shirt up from the floor. I slipped my arms into the shirt and tied a knot with the shirttail to cover my chest. The ticket guy stuffed his cock back in his pants, and we stood for a moment looking at each other.

"So what time do you get off?" I glanced at the textbooks stacked on the candy counter. A student, just as I'd thought.

"After the midnight movie."

I nodded. "And what will you do then?"

He folded his arms over his chest and tilted his head as he regarded me. "Take you out for coffee."

"That's what I thought." I smiled.

That evening was the last time I put on one of my private shows. But it wasn't the last time the ticket guy and I fulfilled each other's fantasies.

RACHEL KRAMER BUSSEL

CHECK, MATE

PULL OUT MY CHAIR and gracefully sit down before the sixty-four-square, black-and-white board, a refined masterpiece imbued with the art of the ancient ritual of chess; taking my place as if I were the queen on the board overseeing her minions, rather than just a decent player going up against worthy competition, with as good a chance as anyone else of coming out ahead. Sometimes that's how I like to think of chess, especially when my opponent is a hot guy who would otherwise make me quake in my pointy heels.

I pretend each tournament is like a ball, an old-fashioned yet elegant battle of the sexes, with each side jockeying for position, eyeing one another up and down, perusing, plotting, percolating, trying to get the better of not only centuries of knowledge but of each other.

Chess is as much about reading people as it is about knights and rooks, a psychological thriller writ large as synapses fire and mind games abound. As with poker, the more you can discern about the other player's style and motives, the better off you'll be as you get into the thick of the game, when a single crucial move can take an hour. It's as much about what happens off the board as on, and I never underestimate the power of a little psychological warfare, not to mention the strategic use of cleavage.

Anything that works, right?

I wear business suits like the one I have on today, sleek, sharp and black, unbuttoned just enough to reveal the swell of my large breasts, which are barely contained by the demi-bra underneath a thin shell of a white top, the kind that costs a hundred dollars to look like it cost five. During the game, I get up and stride through the aisles, my eyes flitting over pieces locked into tangled configurations, elaborate schemes that require the sexiest of all activities: thinking.

When I've returned to my own sliver of intellectual foreplay, I'm back in power mode: *I'm* the queen, *he's* the king, and we're playing until one of us surrenders—or dies. The sexual tension and high stakes ratchet things up a notch for me, and I probably look like I'm fantasizing about something much more exciting than seeing his king boxed into a corner, unable to escape.

I've come to be at least a local chess champion, working my way up through the ranks into the upper echelons of the game, where players speak in code that outsiders cannot penetrate, rattling off moves and names and endings that only make sense to the rarified few. I can take or leave all the insider madness, the posturing and politics; when I'm here, I just want to play, and play hard. When I'm done, I let loose by fucking the hell out of whoever's in my bed.

Reporters have commented on my seemingly lackadaisical approach, suggesting it's a way to lull my opponents into complacency until my killer instinct picks up and I zoom in, battering away at their defenses until they have no choice but to surrender. My pussy clenches with fierce need as I think of his cock throbbing hard as the adrenaline zips through his bloodstream while we both wait for this attack to be fully unfurled. The foreplay as he staves me off, postponing what feels like the inevitable (even though it's not), and the fact that I could topple myself with a wayward move at any moment, giving way to his sly positioning, makes nothing a foregone conclusion. By the time things get really ugly, we're both usually poised to attack, breathing through our noses, sinking further and further into our own interior world. I imagine that our feral play belongs somewhere far less tame than under the overhead fluorescents of some suburban hotel, and think about chess being played by early sages, think of real wars being won or lost at the game's hand. Those who miss the sexual overtones are really missing out, but I'm not an evangelist. Like most things in life, those who want to partake of the erotic side of the game, those whose bodies and minds are always primed to pervert, will call the kinkiness of a chess game immediately. For the others, the power dynamic at play is wasted, the chance to conquer, tease, invade, and capture lost when taken too literally.

I bite my lip and tilt my head just slightly to the side, knowing how my sparkly silver earrings glint in the light, how my carefully coiffed brown hair falls just so. Whether or not I win the game before me, I need to win the one afterward, the one that will get my sexy opponent, him with the light brown hair falling over to cover his blue eyes, the bitten-down nails on the oversize hands, the baggy black shirt that leaves no hint of whether he's buff or bland beneath, into my bed. They stage these competitions at hotels that strive to be four star, but usually peak at two and a half. It's no Soho Grand, but tossing and turning against the crisp, cool sheets while trying to fall asleep last night, I knew I couldn't stand another solo evening and sensed that the right man would soon present himself to me, whether he was aware of it or not.

Fixating on this morning's enemy, knowing I will eventually make him squirm, maybe even tie him to my bed and see what he makes of being bound and helpless, makes me tingle with anticipation. I look to the board, where we're slowly shifting from a Ruy Lopez opening that I, with the white pieces, initiated, to a middlegame that's becoming decidedly murky as we each battle for control. I've been on the offensive but am debating whether to push on full speed ahead or proceed with caution and wait for him to crumble upon himself.

I subtly move a pawn on the side of the board, not giving away a hint of my plans, then press the button on the clock. My mind moves back to what will happen after we're done. For all my fantasizing, I've never actually bedded any of my opponents. I usually pick up men in the bar afterward while enjoying a well-deserved cocktail, men who are more than happy to pound me in ways even the most crushing of chess blows can't do. I've certainly thought about fondling some of the men (not to mention the women) who've sat across from me, especially the ones who've bested me with more than bravado. Being surrounded by so much sheer brainpower is often enough to make me drip as I wonder if some of these men could come close to doing with their bodies what they do with their minds: overpower, attack, pursue, conquer. I picture them chasing me around a bedroom until they pin me down and have their way with me, or switching things up and prostrating themselves before me and allowing me to slowly stroke them to ecstasy. I never picture dainty, demure sex; someone is always screaming and slapping and riding and writhing. I picture a leisurely dance of flirtation, the kind whose power builds the longer it's made to wait, until we rip each other's clothes off and have at it.

From the start, during those minutes of speculation that give me pause, when it's really too early for him to be thinking so hard, and yet he does, he's made me keep looking. I am forced to let my eyes linger on the board as his do, see it through his eyes as well as my own. Usually, the first five moves are blazed through as if by memory, each of us waiting for the other to take things out of the familiar realm, the openings we've studied countless times, into a brave new world where we can't rely on anything but our wits, but this guy knows exactly what he's doing. As his intense eyes dart around the board, seeing possibilities that clearly only exist in his mind, I finally give up trying to second-guess him and focus on possibilities that are only in my mind as I wait for his cue. The pieces will be there when I get back from my mental detour, so I think about him standing before me while I slowly undress, removing layer after layer, just slowly enough to make him wonder what else lies beneath.

As the game gets more complex, we start to draw a crowd, pulled in by the complications we've brought to this uncharted territory. He lifts his hand to move his bishop, his fingers reaching for its phallic head, then pausing there for a moment, as if unsure that his intended choice is a good one. The rule is if you touch it, you move it. But as long as he keeps his fingers there, he can still move it wherever he wants.

If we were on a date and he were deciding what to eat, I might slip my foot out of my shoe and gently glide it up his leg, not helping him make his choice but filling him with desire, nonetheless. Instead, I shift to the side, straining forward enough to let a tiny bit more cleavage show. As his brow furrows, I picture it doing the very same thing as he slides what has to be a fat cock inside me.

Thinking about fucking him not only helps pump me up to win the game, it allows me to mask my true thoughts; I've never had much of a poker face and have blown games when bursts of utter glee raced across my face, causing my opponents to revise their hastily drawn plans. The more he makes me wait, the more tempted I am to blow the game, fold my king in humiliation, sweep the pieces to the floor, and slam him against the wall. His slow manner seems to mock me, as if he feels none of the same urgency.

In my befuddled state, I drop my pen on the ground, and when I bend down to pick it up, I really can't help but look up at his erection. Oh, it's there all right, silently straining against his jeans, thick and solid and all mine. At least, it will be once we get this damn game over with. I sit back up but still feel antsy, twiddling with the pen in my lap. His eyebrows twitch and he bites his lip as his eyes careen around from one side of the board to the next. Eventually, I stand and stroll behind him, looking at the board from his angle, from his side, but even so, I miss what he's been plotting all along. It seems so obvious once I fall into his trap, but until then, I'm utterly confident in my moves.

I have no time to be shocked or fight back; his pieces have already entered my lair. I'm exposed just as surely as if I were strung up spread-eagled, my pussy open and vulnerable. That's what I think about as I tremblingly move my king one short step away from doom. But he comes at me again, this time moving faster, pouncing. A quick glance at his face finds it smooth, unmarked by wrinkles, as my heart pounds at this new development. The onlookers fade from my peripheral vision as we duke it out on the board. A glimmer of an exit path beams at me, but he squelches it in moments until my king stands naked, quivering, and I'm forced to surrender him to the obvious conclusion. Yet I don't feel like I've lost; my brain is on fire, not to mention my pussy.

After I lean my king's head against the board, I offer my hand to my opponent. When our palms meet, I worry that I've let out too loud of an exhale. I quietly help him put the pieces back in their container, wondering if he will scurry off like all the rest. But as I place the last knight in its bag, he grabs my wrist. His thumb presses against the tender underside, his grip surprisingly strong. He tilts his head, indicating he wants to speak with me.

I follow him into the hallway where he pins me against the wall. It's lewd, hot, and nasty, our mashed-together bodies visible to anyone who wants to see. "I think I've won more than that chess game, Laura," he says, pressing his cock against me. It's undeniably hard, and I stare up at his face, so close and intense. "You got me so hard in there I could barely think, and I can tell that you're the kind of girl who needs to pay a price for losing, aren't you?" His fingers graze my nipple gently, but that soft touch is enough to nearly make me slide down the wall, held up by the power of his gaze, and his dick.

"Yes," I say quietly, no longer the power player I'd been even half an hour before. Now I really am his to do with as he pleases, surrendering to him right there as surely as if I'd been playing for my freedom. He pulls me along to the elevator banks, and my cheeks burn as I briefly make eye contact with some of the other players, who look on with curiosity and more than a little intrigue, probably wishing they could join us. But he whisks me into the elevator and just stares at me until we reached his floor. I scurry to keep up with him as he charges ahead, walking so fast that I bump into his backside as he tries to slot the key card into its hole. He reaches behind him and places his hand on my belly. Not my breasts or my pussy, but in between the two, over the buttons of my suit coat, where my body was roiling the most. He holds his fingers there until the door unlocks, then marches forward and sends me lurching after him.

We don't need pleasantries or cocktails or even lights. He pins me roughly to the wall and kisses me, his lips smashing against mine as he rips the jacket off me, sending buttons flying. I've always thought if that happened in real life I'd be pissed, alarmed at the cost and waste and utter disregard for my property, but with him, I simply wait for more. He coils the tank top in his larger hand, tugging at it as if trying to make it disappear, before turning me so he can march me toward the bed.

"Get undressed," he says, pushing me onto the king-sized mattress, his blue eyes darkened with lust. This time I tremble, but without a hint of fear. I know he's about to give me exactly what I want. We aren't living out our chess game but the pent-up desire we've each held in check during it. I strip as fast as I can, leaving a sloppy pile of clothes in my haste.

He unzips his jeans and the dick I'd glimpsed earlier pops out, larger than what I'd expected. Will it be too large? It seems almost monstrous, but then I feel myself quiver. "It's not too big, is it Laura?" he asks, walking toward me and reaching for my hand. The minute I make contact with his cock, I know it isn't too big for any of my holes. I shake, swallow hard, blink back the tears that threaten to fall softly onto the bedspread.

"It's perfect," I tell him, and he turns me around again so I'm bent over the bed, legs spread on the ground, ass in the air, body arched, ready to be invaded. He pulls apart my asscheeks and for a moment I think he's going to try to fuck my ass with his big, bare dick, and I wonder if I'll let him. My breathing becomes fierce and loud, but before I can bite my lip to keep in the sounds, he's plunging his fingers inside me.

"Oh, you're ready, you little slut," he says. Hearing his gravelly voice I let myself become his slut, become the girl with her legs open for a virtual stranger, wooed simply by his skill at moving pieces of carved wood across a glossy board, at outwitting me while I'd had sex on the brain. He adds another finger, and then I hear a condom wrapper being opened. I arch backward, raising my ass as high as it will go, and then he's inside me, that huge dick taking what I'm giving him, giving me back a rush of excitement. I fuck him, rocking my hips as I try to get him even deeper inside. He holds me down by the small of my back, pushing me until I can't move, must simply lie there and let him slam and slide and surge and collide into my tight cunt. I am no longer the queen or even a lowly pawn; I am a wayward peasant caught by a vicious guard, "made" to give myself to him even though I've dreamed of such a capture since I was a little girl.

He seems to sense that I need more, need it all, need his cock and then some, because he moves me aside and bends me over so my hands are planted on the floor, my hair hanging down, as he drills into me. His hands move to my asscheeks, squeezing and pinching them, and that, joined with his fat cock's relentless rhythm, makes me scream so loud I startle even myself. It's the scream I've held in every time I've gone for dainty over dick-mad, sweet over slutty, coy over cock-crazed.

I scream like he's playing the ultimate game of life with me, playing my body with as sure strokes as his moves with the black and white pieces. He doesn't speak or try to silence me or even react all that much, but his dick is louder than even my cries. I eventually slow down, sobbing my way to a vicious orgasm that seems to last for minutes, as only the sound of my slickness being speared again and again fills my ears. Wordlessly, he takes me to the place where I am all woman, all pussy, all sex, a place I've needed to go for so long but have had to wait for the right transportation to get me there. His cock is my vessel, my ride, my fantasy come true, and I let him plow me like that until it seems like my pussy might burst with pleasure. I don't know how many times I come, just that I am so slick his dick keeps sliding out, making him hold me ever tighter.

When he pushes my hips forward just enough to slide his cock out, I moan with part relief, part sadness. My body has clung to his, getting used to his shape inside me. He kneels down and licks at my sex, his tongue gentle in all the ways his dick hadn't been, and he sucks me to another climax that really does make me cry. It's like a lullaby after a rock anthem, a gentle letdown. Then he pulls me around so my face is in his lap, the condom off, my lips sucking him slowly, gently. He doesn't rush me either, knowing that this blow job is as much for me as for him. With tears still streaking my face, he cradles me in his lap as I coax the come out of him, too spent for a spirited up and down. He strokes my hair while I slowly work his mega-dick. When he finally comes, I have to ease back and let some of his juice drip down my chin, swallowing what I can until he is done.

I lie there with my head in his lap, his come drying on my face, suffused with his smell, the room still charged with our energy. When I finally open my eyes, the room is dark and my head is on a pillow. I sit up slowly so as not to jerk myself out of my bliss too fast. I look at the bed to find a chessboard perfectly arranged, the elegant pieces of what must have been a pricey set glinting before me by the light of a lamp.

"Ready for a rematch?" he asks, holding a piece behind each hand, the traditional way of choosing who goes first. I point to his right hand and grin.

NINE BALL, CORNER POCKET

GRIN ON HIS FACE, Jesse leaned against the wall, his legs crossed at the ankles. A cue stood to attention in front of his groin, gripped between strong, folded arms. Across the pool table, Rhiannon leaned down and lined up her shot. The tip of her tongue licked between her lips as she concentrated.

"Two ball to the nine, corner pocket," she said.

Jesse spared the table a quick glance before giving a soft, derisive snort.

Glaring, Rhiannon's eyes lifted to his. "Don't think I can make it?"

"Not a chance, honey," was his self-satisfied response.

"Oh, really?" She pulled away from the table, striking her "I can't believe you're doubting me" stance.

Jesse snorted again. He was accustomed to her moods and poses. When it came to pool, he was also familiar with her abilities, or rather, lack of them. After all, they'd played many similar games at his home, on the same table. They'd also played a different kind of sport, fucking each other senseless on its emerald-green velvet. He could almost hear the tiny whimpers in her throat as she climaxed, her sweet juices running down her legs as he pounded into her from behind.

"Care to make a wager on that?" she snapped, interrupting his sordid thoughts.

Jesse was startled, realizing he hadn't heard what she'd said. He asked her to repeat herself. When she did, he grinned. "Ria, I'm not going to take your money."

"I meant something more wicked than money."

Intrigued, he pushed off from the wall and stepped toward the pool table, leaning on its edge. "How wicked?"

"How about if I miss this shot, you get to fuck my tight little ass?"

Straining to think straight at her announcement, Jesse wondered what the catch was. "And if you make the shot?" was his faintly suspicious reply.

Quick as a whip, she retorted, "I get to watch you get your tight little ass fucked." Her amusement was rapidly increasing.

Bingo, there was the catch, although somehow, it didn't seem such a bad trade. Rhiannon had been hinting about wanting to watch him and another man for a while, ever since he'd confessed his interest in gay porn. Her idea contained a certain dark appeal.

Before he lost his nerve, he agreed to her sinful dare. "You're on, babe, but on one condition: if you win, I still get to fuck your tight little ass sometime soon, just the way you've always wanted."

Rhiannon nodded and then leaned down to line up her shot

again. A sharp glance in Jesse's direction convinced him not to cheat. Sometimes, he was in the habit of startling her with a sudden noise. She was well versed in his underhand tactics. Gripping the cue loosely, she slid it back and forth between her fingers, watching him out of the corner of her eye. Again, the tip of her tongue licked between her lips as she briefly caught sight of his squirm.

Drawing the cue back, she slid it slowly forward again, almost tapping the cue ball. Focusing her attention again on the shot, she widened her stance, took a deep breath, and slowly swung her arm back.

As the cue slid forward between her fingers, Rhiannon held her breath and prayed. The two ball gently tapped the nine and, for a moment, it hugged the rim, before falling into the pocket. In that moment, Jesse knew Rhiannon had triumphed. He only hoped that in the end, he'd win as well.

After her victory, Rhiannon planted a quick kiss on Jesse's lips and then headed home for the night, leaving him to dwell on what was to come.

Jesse brooded over his position as he sat in front of the TV, intently watching several rented videos showing gay men in various erotic situations. For two days, he rushed home from work, first checking his answering machine, before playing a video and lubricating his hands.

He masturbated to scenes of construction workers, college roommates, and military men, but his favorite movie featured two men in a pool hall. He stroked his cock raw as he repeatedly watched one man bugger the other with the butt end of a pool cue, before the cue wielder fucked his willing victim.

It gave Jesse an added thrill when he pressed a finger inside his ass, wriggling it as he jerked himself off. He'd even been tempted to try something a bit firmer and bigger, like the minivibrator Rhiannon kept in the nightstand, but he hadn't been able to work up the nerve.

As evening fell on the third day, Jesse heard his cell phone ring and he glanced at the display. Rhiannon had finally decided to call. As he answered, loud techno-music assaulted his ears. He could barely hear Rhiannon's shouts, but eventually he made out what she was saying.

"I'll be at your place in about an hour. Wear those jeans of yours I like and nothing else, and make sure you have the lube and a few condoms handy."

A click sounded in his ear as the loud music and Rhiannon's voice were replaced by a dial tone. His hand suddenly shaking, Jesse closed his cell and then rushed to pick up the clutter in his apartment before company arrived.

An hour later, he'd just finished clearing the mess when the doorbell rang.

Closing the dishwasher and flicking the switch, he surveyed the apartment as he headed to the front door. The rented videos were hidden, the couch cushions were flipped over, and he'd moved the lube into the bedroom. The tube now sat on the dresser, next to a full box of condoms. Everything looked normal, except he was wearing jeans that were slightly baggy over his hips, no boxers, no shirt—and he was about to have sex with a man he'd never met.

Forcing a smile to his lips, he concentrated on steadying his hand; first one deep breath, then another. Closing his eyes, he pictured Rhiannon leaning over the pool table, her legs spread and her asshole lubed and ready. Glancing at his hand again, he noticed it was steady, but he also caught sight of the increasing bulge in his jeans. With a nervous flourish, Jesse opened the door to the wonders that were to come.

Jesse's eyes widened as they trailed over Rhiannon's "friend." It only took a moment for him to realize he knew Neil, though normally Rhiannon's editor was dressed in a nice suit and sported slicked-back hair. He oozed heterosexual vibes and turned many a feminine head.

Yet the man standing in front of him was rugged, dressed in tight jeans and a white T-shirt. His tattoos were clearly visible and a very noticeable hard-on strained against the seam of his jeans.

"Jesse, I hear I get to pop your cherry," Neil taunted. He placed a hand against Jesse's chest and gently pushed him back into the apartment. Slowly sliding his hand down his willing victim's torso to the waist of his jeans, he hooked his finger in a belt loop and pulled the unresisting man toward him.

Rhiannon closed the door behind them.

"Between you and me, I think I'm going to love every minute of it. I have a feeling you will as well."

Jesse gulped silently and opened his mouth to respond, but he never got a chance. Neil leaned forward and pressed his lips to his, sparking sudden feral desire. Almost instantly, Jesse felt his cock get even stiffer. Unfulfilled fantasies began to roar through his mind. The texture of those male lips was similar to Rhiannon's but different somehow. They were firmer and more impatient.

Neil took possession of Jesse's mouth, thrusting his tongue past willingly parted lips. The insistent organ searched out its wet and warm opposite number. Neil's hands slid around Jesse's hips, pulling the shell-shocked man against him.

Jesse admired this display of dominance, even as he submitted. Groin to groin with the other man now, Jesse ground his hips slowly, igniting a trail of need in them both.

Behind them, Rhiannon watched intently as her best friend and her lover dueled for control.

Jesse saw Neil pull back to look at him, and he knew what Neil would see because Rhiannon had told him often enough. Neil would notice the way his hair spiked slightly; he'd notice a crescent of thick lashes lying against tanned cheeks. Jesse understood his own qualities, the perfect working-class construction worker, toned, tanned, and sexy as hell.

As Jesse's eyes locked on Neil's, his seducer leaned down and kissed him again. At that moment, Jesse noticed the light floral scent of Rhiannon's perfume. She'd moved to stand beside him. He felt her carefully grasp his hand.

Half directing, half pulling, Rhiannon led the two men to the bedroom. She wanted them comfortable, at ease.

Jesse allowed himself to be guided backward, Rhiannon setting the pace.

As the door closed with a soft click, Jesse pulled away from Neil. For a second, the sensual haze cleared from his mind and the true reality of his situation dawned. Panic began to creep in.

"I can't do this," he whispered, his eyes darting to Rhiannon.

"Shhh, baby," she whispered, stepping between the two men. Raising her hands to Jesse's chest, she also nodded slightly toward Neil, before turning back to reassure her boyfriend. "Nothing's going to happen that you don't want."

Slowly twining her fingers in the soft golden curls covering her lover's chest, she coaxed his lips down to hers. They kissed passionately, as her hands roamed over his ribs, down to the well-worn buttons of his Levi's. Undoing them, she slipped his jeans over his ass and let gravity take effect.

Kneeling down at Jesse's ankles and gently grasping, she lifted his feet one after the other, until he'd stepped out of the worn, blue garment. "Just relax, baby, and let me take care of you," she said as she straightened up a little and looked toward his handsome face.

With a quick flick of her tongue to dampen her lips, she leaned forward slightly and kissed the head of his cock. A small drop of precome oozed to the tip and she teased him, swirling her tongue over the glistening drop, before sucking his length into her mouth. She tasted an inch, then pulled back, each delay driving him wild. Another inch, then again she backed off.

Slowly, sensually, she aroused him to fever pitch. His hands twisted in her perfectly done-up hair, pulling the pins free and leaving her long tresses dangling down her back. Soon, he forgot all about the other man in the room, watching his beautiful siren have her way with his willing flesh.

Her hands tenderly cupped his ball sac, playing gently with the sensitive skin. Moaning softly, he arched into her mouth, thrusting his cock in a steady rhythm. Muted sucking sounds filled the room, his groans a low accompaniment.

As Ria pulled back, he could hear the sound of her mouth on his flesh and his eyes flickered open. He saw Neil standing to his left, naked. Only the occasional tattoo covered his tanned flesh. Then Neil's ink-black eyes met his and Jesse couldn't look away, even when Rhiannon's satiny mouth moved back over his straining erection.

He watched, fascinated, as Neil cupped his own cock and gently stroked himself. Desperately, Jesse wanted to feel it pound into him and stretch him to his limits. His fears were soon forgotten when Rhiannon's mouth drove him back to the brink, before she suddenly pulled away again.

Now, he watched as her lovely lips closed around Neil's cock, sucking it deep within her warm, velvety mouth. Jealousy pulsed inside him as he gazed. He wanted to taste Neil's flesh as well.

Dropping to his knees, he gently pushed Rhiannon away and moved to take her place. Hesitantly, he kissed Neil's stiffness, tasting the salty essence leaking from the bulging tip. Taking a deep breath, he opened his lips and sucked the inviting phallus deep into his mouth. For a moment, he gagged, then backed off, remembering past girlfriends and their tentative attempts. Trying again, he took Neil's erection more deeply into his mouth and then pulled back.

Softly, Neil's hands came to rest on Jesse's head, guiding him without pressure until he found a comfortable rhythm.

Jesse's eyes now focused completely on Neil, watching for subtle clues. He wasn't sure what to do next. When Neil's lids fluttered closed, and his Adam's apple bobbed, Jesse knew he was doing okay. Filled with confidence, he sucked harder, stroking his hands up and down Neil's thighs, enjoying the feel of the wiry hair beneath his palms.

Jesse knew Neil was close to orgasm when he felt his hands tighten in his hair. He knew because, when Rhiannon went down on him, he reacted the same way, holding her face still as he fucked her throat.

Jesse watched as Neil's eyes opened suddenly and his nostrils flared a little. Then, out of the corner of his eye, he saw what had drawn Neil's attention away. Rhiannon was slowly undressing, her hands running over her stomach and thighs, caressing her smooth skin. For a moment, his hands itched to return to his sweet love's softness, but as drops of pre-come leaked from Neil's slit, Jesse returned his attention to his male paramour.

Rhiannon watched, half dazed, as Jesse sucked Neil deep into his mouth. She couldn't quite believe her fantasy, their fantasy, was coming true. Wanting to make the moment last as long as possible, she slowly returned to removing her white shirt and leather skirt.

Only her heels, hose, and garter remained as she knelt, once again, next to Jesse. Carefully lying on her stomach, she shifted as close to him as possible and then softly parted his asscheeks, sliding her tongue along the cleft. The forbidden crevice was tangy with sweat; it almost seemed to beckon her.

Ria knew Neil was watching her closely as she experienced this delight for the first time—and his mesmerized eyes made her shiver with pleasure.

Suddenly, she felt Jesse jerk and she watched as Neil soothed him—tenderly brushing his hands over her boyfriend's face and shoulder. He quickly guided Jesse back into a steady rhythm, as Ria also prepared her lover for the wonders to come.

Minutes passed as the three reveled in their exploration. Then Rhiannon decided to move things to the next stage. She pulled away from Jesse and stood. Stepping between the two men to draw their attention, she moved toward the bedside table and grabbed the tube of lubricant, squeezing some into her palm.

She rubbed her hands together to warm the cool gel, before carefully spreading it between her buttocks. Gritting her teeth at the slight discomfort, she forced a finger inside her anus as far as she could reach.

She jumped a little, as another hand joined hers. Pulling her finger free, she allowed Neil to coat his own two digits and then thrust them deep into her ass. With his other hand, he guided her onto her belly across the bed, her feet planted firmly on the floor.

Jesse watched as Neil forced his fingers in and out of her butt, gently twisting them as he did. Rhiannon was intrigued by the look on her lover's face, as her ass fought a bit against the invasion. Small streams of fire flooded her nerves, but she was careful not to show her discomfort.

"Spread your legs further," Neil demanded, as he settled his body between her silky thighs. His palm firmly planted against her back, he pinned her legs against the bed with his and continued to fuck her with his fingers. The fire soon turned into an inferno, as her flesh responded to this sensual invasion. She loved the feel of Neil's weight against her body. Being pinned to the bed and speared on his fingers made her feel incredibly wicked.

Arching her hips, she lifted her body from the bed, so she could move her hand down to her quivering clit and bring it some relief. Her emotions whirled, as Neil finger-fucked her virgin ass. Her boyfriend stood by and let him, his hands slowly stroking his own cock. Rhiannon gave in, closing her eyes.

Instantly, the sensations intensified until she couldn't contain herself any longer. Arching and bucking against Neil, she timed her fingers' thrusts to his until, together, they fucked her into a quivering orgasm.

Trembling and weak, she collapsed against the bed and opened her eyes as a weight settled next to her. Jesse lay there, his eyes locked on her face as he slowly reached back and parted his asscheeks.

Returning his soft smile, Rhiannon forced her limbs to move and settled herself against the headboard. Grabbing a condom from the dresser, she waited patiently.

Jesse couldn't quite believe he'd parted his own asscheeks, but as Neil moved behind him and slid the tip of the lubricant tube into his ass, he no longer cared. His body demanded satisfaction, even as his mind rebelled. He knew there would be discomfort and maybe even pain.

Watching Rhiannon's face had underlined that fact. He knew her well enough to know she'd tried to hide it. He also knew he had nerves in that sensitive area that a woman didn't. If Rhiannon had adjusted, and even enjoyed it, he could only imagine what he would feel.

Taking a deep breath, he tried to prepare for the sensation of a handful of cool gel inside his ass. When he experienced it, he trembled as he anticipated what was to follow.

He sensed Neil shift away, and he turned his head when he heard foil rustling. He saw Neil standing next to Rhiannon; she was sliding a condom over his weeping cock. Other than the sweet spread of Ria's pussy lips, he wondered if he'd ever seen a more erotic sight. Her dainty hands slid over the latex-coated flesh, spreading a layer of lube over Neil's eager erection. Her eyes met Jesse's, and she smiled her gentle siren's smile.

Unable to stand the suspense, his fingers clenched the sheets and he closed his eyes. The feel of gentle hands on his ass made him tremble. Neil moved to stand against him, reminiscent of the way he'd pinned Ria down. A palm pressed against his back, and Jesse took a deep breath.

"Relax." Neil's cultured tones contrasted sharply with the motifs that decorated his body. For a moment, Jesse wondered what had motivated Neil. He'd been tattooed at least six different times.

Relaxing, as a fingernail tapped against his anus, Jesse took a deep breath. Then a long finger slipped past his ring. Soon it was joined by a second. Slowly, they worked in and out of his ass, pushing against the ring of nerves. Twitching slightly, Jesse arched back into the touch.

It was like nothing he'd ever felt before. He had always been tempted to include ass play in his sex life, but before Rhiannon, no other woman had been interested. Rhiannon was willing to fuck his ass with a strap-on, but first she wanted him to be fully breached by a man. With that lucky pool shot, she'd made her requirement a reality and fulfilled a fantasy for them both.

Lost in the sensations, with sparks of pleasure racing throughout his body, he didn't at first notice the pressure had eased. The first touch of Neil's cock against his ass ring quickly brought his attention back to the present. Trying to relax was hard.

"Wait a moment, Neil." Rhiannon's soft voice stilled the pressure against Jesse's ass. Opening his eyes, Jesse watched Ria settle in front of him. She knelt, with her legs parted. Reaching down, she separated her slick pussy lips and the scent of her arousal flooded his senses.

Dipping her fingers deeply, she coated them in her juices and spread the smooth essence of her arousal on Jesse's lips. Licking the sweetness, he closed his eyes and savored the moment.

Distracted, he didn't notice Neil pressing against his ring, until Neil's glans had slipped inside him. A moment passed, and he felt a curious stretching sensation as Neil's cock completely penetrated his ass. Gritting his teeth, he waited for the pain, but there wasn't much. As Neil moved within him, Jesse's fists gripped the sheets and he followed his lover's rhythm. Within moments, they were working together in a steady thrust, then withdrawal.

Rhiannon watched as her lover's ass was fucked swift and hard. Her favorite fantasy was playing out before her eyes. Some night soon, she knew her own butt would open for Jesse's cock. Until then, she planned to enjoy watching Jesse being ass-fucked.

Thrusting two fingers deep into her pussy, she used her other hand to play with her clit. Both hands soon grew wet with her juices as she fucked herself into another orgasm. Trembling and crying when her climax eventually arrived, she collapsed beside Jesse as his howls of pleasure filled the room.

Clenching at each of Neil's thrusts, Jesse ground his hips against the soft sheets. His cock steadily leaked pre-come and his balls tightened. Jesse knew it was all about to end. He was about to orgasm with a man's cock sawing in and out of his ass. With each thrust, his erection rubbed against the soft sheets. With each withdrawal, his ass begged for more.

Thrust and withdrawal, grind and clench. Over and over, the two lovers worked against, then with each other, drawing both of them closer to the inevitable.

Animalistic grunts echoed off the walls, but Jesse was too far gone to notice the sounds were coming from his own mouth.

His ass begged for each hard thrust and his cock pulsed with need. Balls tight, he ground his hips against the sheets as Neil pushed deep inside him. Clenching his lover tightly, he locked his legs and jerked against the sheets. Weird sensations wracked his body as he climaxed. Hot, sticky squirts shot from his throbbing flesh, creating a warm, tacky pool on the bed. Convulsing with each spurt of his orgasm, he clenched tighter, pulling Neil into the vortex.

Closing his eyes, Jesse arched against Neil as his new lover pounded into him. Within moments, Neil's slight weight collapsed onto Jesse's back. Vaguely, Jesse heard Rhiannon gasp as she climaxed a third time. All that mattered was the steadily softening cock in his ass, the weight of a man lying on him, and the come leaking from his own cock.

With a soft sigh, he shifted, forcing Neil to roll off. With sleepy eyes, he watched as Neil pulled the latex from his cock and tossed it in the trash. Jesse slid toward Rhiannon, making room for Neil on the bed. Pressing his face against Ria's moist flesh, Jesse took a deep breath as he struggled to bring sanity to a world made up entirely of tingling nerves.

"Mmmmm," he managed, as Rhiannon nuzzled her pussy against his lips.

Tentatively, he stuck his tongue out and wiggled it as she ground against him. Her fingers occasionally brushed against his forehead. As he gradually collected his thoughts, his limbs still deliciously lethargic, Jesse rolled over just enough for Ria to mount his face and grind herself to another screaming orgasm.

The bed dipped as Neil settled beside him, and Jesse shifted in response, spooning with his new lover. Within moments, Rhiannon had joined them, snuggling her back against Jesse's chest.

Lying there, the three held each other as they adjusted to the changes one night had caused. Jesse wasn't certain how Neil was going to fit into their relationship, but the fact Rhiannon had chosen him, instead of any number of bi and gay men she knew, spoke volumes. He knew Rhiannon had been attracted to her editor since day one and that, despite their attraction, they had become good friends.

Jesse felt Neil smile against his neck, but he wasn't quite sure why.

Rhiannon yawned, her body humming with contentment. Remembering the bet with Neil that started it all, she couldn't help but smile. She could never have guessed her pool lessons with Neil would pay off so well. As her eyes drifted shut, images of the future filled her mind. She knew that soon Neil would demand her ass, as well as Jesse's, preferably while bent over the pool table—as per their agreement at the beginning of her tutorial in the sport. She had the distinct feeling Jesse was going to enjoy everything she and Neil had planned for him.

BROOKE STERN

UNFINISHED BUSINESS

GOING TO TRADE SHOWS had never been Alex's thing. He looked around the convention hall. They all looked the same. He was tempted to turn around, go back to his hotel room, and read a book or something, but then he felt a tap on his shoulder.

"Remember me?"

She was stunning. Short blonde hair, fashionable black suit, crisp white blouse buttoned up to her neck. She didn't look like anyone else there. At shows like this, the buyers tended to be older men and the vendors' booths were fronted by cute young women for the buyers to ogle. What this arrangement lacked in dignity it made up for in efficacy, and Alex had become accustomed to it by now. He always wondered if there was some rent-a-model temp agency that the vendors used to staff their booths. While unbearably cute, these girls were all too young and insubstantial for him.

The woman standing before him, however, was a bit older and more sophisticated. He had thought she looked familiar but had dismissed the possibility that he knew her as wishful thinking. Yet here she was, smiling knowingly while she awaited his answer. Alex had the horrible feeling that she was about to get the best of him. He tried to place her but failed. He was confident that he would remember if any of his professional connections looked like her. Blonde hair. He had never even been on a date with a blonde. Cute smile and eyes that looked at him with encouragement.

"Are you a movie star? Because I don't get to the movies much."

As soon as he said it, Alex regretted making it into a game.

"Come on, Alex. You don't need to be embarrassed. I'm the one who asked for it."

Shit. Sarah. Dyed hair. New clothes. A year older. Not bent over his lap with her panties around her ankles.

"Oh, my God. Sarah. It's so good to see you." He tried to cover his embarrassment with enthusiasm.

"Yeah, you too, Alex."

Awkward pause.

"So how have you been?"

"Fine. You?"

"Good. Good."

Whatever. They looked at each other blankly for a moment before Alex couldn't help but ask what was really on his mind.

"Aren't you mad at me?"

"Why should I be?"

"You tell me. I never understood why you left."

"Jesus, Alex. It wasn't any big deal. I just had to go, that's all. It freaked me out a little, but it's not like there was anything wrong with it."

That wasn't how Alex remembered it. He remembered the drink, the flirting, the coy spanking references, and then he remembered more drinks, more flirting, and more spanking references, until they finally ended up in his hotel room, ready to realize their fantasies. But he also remembered her storming out, barely taking the time to pull up her panties, let alone offer an explanation.

Standing before him now, Sarah resembled Ms. Model Citizen. She gave the impression that she couldn't have been pried out of her buttoned-up suit by Casanova with a roofie. Her prim composure looked impenetrable. It was the kind of façade that made Alex sure of two things: first, that he would give anything to spank the look of aloof indifference off her face; and, second, that she would never in a million years consent to anything of the sort. He stared at her and wondered how this could be the same woman who had been more than willing, who had even proposed it, only to abandon it abruptly for no perceptible reason.

But it was definitely the same woman. The woman who stood before him possessed the ass that he had fantasized about almost every day for a year. Behind the fragile beauty of that face—porcelain-like in color and, Alex imagined, porcelain-like in delicacy—lurked the same unforgivable thoughts, appetites, and needs that burned inside him. Which could only mean one thing: that she would want it again this year. Appetites like that don't go away.

"Come with me," Alex said, made bold by the realization. "We can finish what we started."

"I have a meeting in an hour. How about tomorrow night after the reception?"

It changed from an impulse to a premeditated crime. He worried that she would lose her nerve, but he accepted her invitation.

"See you there."

The next night at the reception, Sarah saw Alex from across the room and surprised him again.

"Don't I know you?"

"You look familiar," Alex replied.

"Maybe you saw me in the 2004 romantic comedy *Drinking Alone at a Hotel Bar.*"

This game again? Alex played along.

"Weren't you also in *The Amazing Disappearing Woman?*"

"That wasn't one of my better roles."

"I've been hoping you would do something new."

"Oh, yeah? Any ideas?"

"How about *Unfinished Business?*"

"What's my role?"

"Just be yourself. You'll be fine."

"When does shooting start?"

"After this thing ends. Room eight-seven-three. Let yourself in."

Alex offered her his card key and knew the whole game rested on her response. She took it, turned, and walked away without looking at him. It was a small thing that meant a lot.

The game had worked. It got them where they needed to go, but Alex found the playfulness incongruent with what he was feeling. Was she making it into some funny director-actress game because she was nervous, or was she trying to duck the truth about her running away? Was their gamesmanship a way to ease them into an intense encounter with their secrets, or was it a way to avoid facing them head-on?

The truth was that he still burned from their last encounter. He had spent a year wondering if he had done something terribly wrong. When she cut it short and ran out of his room, she had suddenly seemed erratic, dangerous even. He had worried about what she might do. He had even worried that he might make the same mistake—whatever it was—with other women. Since that night, whenever he was with a woman and remembered how things had gone so badly so fast, he became perceptibly more timid. As much as he fantasized about Sarah, he also resented her, wanting to continue the spanking, only this time he was motivated by a feeling of having really been wronged. Where the original spanking was to fulfill a mutual desire, this one would be to actually punish her for how she had made him feel.

The paradox in punishing a bad behavior by fulfilling a lifelong desire wasn't lost on Alex. But in the deep, sometimes backward, emotional logic of adult, erotic discipline, it made sense. He also understood that the intense, messed-up logic of it might be the very thing that drove her off. It was scary. They were doing something of significance.

Her reluctance to trust a stranger was pitted against her strongest desire; her autonomy was pitted against her hunger to submit, and the need she felt for an intense experience was pitted against her fear of vulnerability and shame. Of course she felt conflicted about what she was doing. Who wouldn't? Last year, she had balked at giving up all control, not only the control over the punishment but also the control she normally exerted over her own emotions. Giving up these controls had triggered some alarm deep inside her. The panic had surprised her as much as it had surprised Alex. Even more surprising to her was that when she tried to bury the panic, her famous self-control had abandoned her and she had just made it out the door before she lost it completely, crying the whole elevator ride back to her room and for much of the next year.

Alex didn't know that Sarah, too, hoped to exorcise some demons that had haunted her ever since. All he knew was that this time it would be different.

Using his card key and letting herself in meant she was doing it of her own accord. She stood outside the door, screwing up her courage and wondering what it meant that she was doing this. What would it mean if she went through with it this time? What would it mean if she didn't?

Alex had been right: there was something that needed finishing. She slid the card key in the slot and stared at the green light before forcing herself to turn the handle.

Alex sat at the desk across the room. It felt like forever before he looked up.

"Hi. I was told that you were looking for an actress for your film."

Her voice revealed more uncertainty than before. Was this the right thing to say? Was this game going to continue? Alex hadn't expected it to. He had expected contrition, some real acknowledgment of what had happened. He considered demanding that she apologize, but it occurred to him that playing along might be the quickest way to get there.

"Are you here to audition?"

"Yeah. I guess."

"What's your name?"

"Sarah Miller."

"What role are you auditioning for?"

"For the girl?"

"Which girl?"

"You know. The girl who…"

Her voice gave way on her, and Alex let her stand awkwardly with the silence for a moment.

"Yes? The girl who…?"

"The girl who has come back."

"Come back, Sarah? I don't understand."

According to the rules of this game, he could play dumb and make her explain.

"I'm the girl with unfinished business."

"That's pretty vague. What business?"

"I'm the girl who wanted to be with a man, but then got scared and left."

"And now you've come back?"

"Yes."

"Are you scared?"

"Yes."

"What are you scared of?"

"Myself."

"Why?"

"I don't know, Alex. I'm just scared. I don't know what I'm going to do."

"I think you're too scared for the role, Sarah."

"No, Alex. Stop doing this. It's not funny anymore."

"It's your game, Sarah. I don't even know if you want to be real."

"I want to be real. I do."

"Then tell me why you're here."

"I can't talk about it, Alex. Just do it to me. Please just do it to me."

"Just do what, Sarah?"

Silence. The rules of the game were very strict. It was her move. Alex couldn't move for her.

"Say it, Sarah, or I can't help you."

"Spank me."

He was testing her, seeing if she would let it play out. If she was going to run, she would do so now. He watched and waited, still behind the desk, using all his strength to remain still and look at her. The truth was, he would have lacked this control if it weren't for the game they had slipped into. Without the game, he would have comforted her, not driven her harder. In the game, though, he could watch, impassive, as the battle waged inside her.

Then she ran, but not toward the door. No, she ran to him. He stood up and caught her in his arms, enveloping her as she collapsed on him and sobbed into his chest. It was a year's worth of tears that had only just begun.

"There, there, honey. Just so you know what kind of movie this is. Now I'd like you to read a scene with me. Come on, sweetheart. Get ahold of yourself."

It was hard for Sarah to stop crying when she felt like she was sinking deeper and deeper into the place that terrified her. She held on to Alex, looking up at him through teary eyes. Could she let herself go so completely with him? He cradled her head in his hand and stroked her hair. It was a gesture that made her feel safe.

"We're going to do the spanking scene. We'll start after you've arrived. You've come back to be punished for running away from the hero. You know that he's glad to have you back, but you also know that you have to face the consequences of the damage you've done. He holds you in his arms as you cry, overcome by regret and fear. How you wish you had never left him, and how you wish you didn't have to get your spanking! You're sorry, but he can only forgive you if he gets to show you how much it hurt. What you've done has torn him up, and now he needs to make you endure the pain that you put him through. Can you understand that, Sarah?"

"Yes."

"He's going to make you take off your skirt and pull down your panties. Then he'll bend you over his lap and spank your bare bottom until your tears are all cried out. He knows that you ran away because you were scared that you couldn't take it. This time, you'll want to run away, but you won't be able to. He'll show you that you can take so much more than you think. He'll make you take it, Sarah. No matter how many times you give up or beg or resist, he'll make you take it."

"But I'm sorry, Alex. I'm so, so sorry. It can't be that harsh. I won't make it. I won't be able to. It'll be like last year. I don't want to fail again. I don't want to disappoint you again. Please don't make it so bad. I'm sorry. I won't do it again. I promise. I really do."

"Take off your skirt, Sarah, and pull down your panties. It's time for your spanking."

"But please, Alex. I was so happy to see you. Let's make it a happy day. Let's not ruin it."

"I'm not ruining it, Sarah. I'm saving it. I'm saving it from what you did last year."

"But why would I come back if it was going to hurt so much?"

"I don't know, Sarah. It's your character. You tell me."

"She wants to close that chapter. She wants to put the unfinished business behind her. But why can't he just understand how hard it is for her?"

"I think she needs more than understanding. If understanding were all she needed, she wouldn't be here. You need to be more honest about these things, Sarah. Your case for leniency is unconvincing. In fact, I'm not sure you know your character at all."

"I know she doesn't want to get the spanking you described. It's more than anyone could want."

"That's bullshit, Sarah. She's fantasized about this spanking her whole life. You're just too scared to go that deep inside her. You're too cowardly to find out what it's like."

His words stung. They hit home with Sarah—she had been called "too scared" before—and she did the only thing she knew to prove him wrong. She took off her skirt and lowered her panties so that the elastic waistband cut into her thighs. *Cowardly? Go to hell.*

"I'm ready. Show me what it's like."

The bravery was an act, a fuck-you to Alex's arrogant judgment. Who was he to tell her what her problem was? He didn't even know her.

But he did. He was right: she had wanted this her whole life, and she had run away last year because she was scared to go this deep and the only thing left for her to do was this.

Like fastening her seat belt before the roller coaster ride, bending over Alex's lap was the last act that Sarah would do of her own volition. It was an irreversible commitment. It was her last move. She felt him grip her firmly—having obviously learned his lesson last year—and she recognized that she had passed the point of no return.

The intellectual realization was one thing, but the physical sensation of Alex's hand landing on her bare flesh was another. The way that patch of pale, tender skin stung changed everything. It felt as if her ass, so long the object of fantasy spankings, had come to be the center of her being. Now all she felt was the agonizing fire that raged as the spanking continued. The pain quickly made her frantic. She squirmed, wriggled, and kicked—anything to slow down the rain of slaps, anything to protect the raw skin where his last blow had just landed.

But even though she was struggling, she wasn't trying to run away. Something about this was right. This was where she was meant to be. She wanted desperately for the pain to stop, but there was something compelling about the sensation. The pain focused her completely. It was clean, like sharp glass, and cut through all the confusion that clouded her head. She could forget about all the negotiations and compromises, all the speculation and guesswork that went into human relations. Typically, the complexity of it all burdened her and took her away from the here and now. Typically, the present only revealed past mistakes or informed future decisions, so that she was always straddling the present, thinking more about the should-have-dones and the must-dos than what she was actually doing.

The spanking demanded she forget all that. The future and past collapsed into the stinging intensity of the present. Even her worries about how she would stand the rest of the spanking were beaten out of her, literally. She could only think of one thing: the pain.

Everything else was so complicated. This was simple.

For Alex, her spanking was an unexpectedly reflective time. He had questions about the spanking. Should he hit the same spot again and again or vary his target, working his way up and down each cheek from her thigh to the top of her crack? How many spanks should he deliver to one cheek before he switched to the other? How often should he take breaks? What was a fair punishment? Was he trying to make it hurt more or not hurt too much?

In typical Alex fashion, he placed his faith in the golden mean and basically split the difference whenever possible.

He found so many aspects of the spanking arousing. Sarah's ass was spectacular, and the view of further treasures between her legs was even better. The shades of red and blotches of emerging bruises were as thrilling to watch as her gasps, moans, and sighs were to hear. He liked the squealing, pleading, and crying, but they diminished as the spanking progressed, and somehow he understood that Sarah was too deep inside herself to make a big display of her feelings, no matter how intense.

More than anything, though, Alex was struck by how well the director-actress game had fit. It was a spur-of-the-moment invention, and he had worried that it would feel too contrived. He worried, too, that it would be a cop-out, a way to avoid owning up to his responsibility for this. But that's not how it felt at all.

A good director breathes life into a scene, and that was what Alex was doing. The role-playing had answered the question of how a bunch of scripted lines—"You've been a very naughty girl," "You need a spanking," "No, please don't spank me on the bare bottom"—could feel anything but hackneyed and clichéd. It had allowed him to deliver lines like these without feeling ridiculous, without feeling like a sleazy pervert or a Victorian headmaster wannabe.

Yes, it was a game, but the old acting adage felt true: sometimes you can only be yourself when you're playing. This was where Sarah and Alex could be themselves. Alex was the man bringing his hand down hard on her exposed ass, while Sarah, beyond herself with pain, felt as urgent a need for this to continue as she felt for it to end. When it ended, this part of them would be forced to recede into the deep places in their heads where it lived, secretly, stowed away in their otherwise normal lives. Neither of them wanted to return to their normal lives.

Not yet.

Impact is to spanking as friction is to sex. Anyone who thinks that a hand spanking is the mild cousin of canes, paddles, and belts has never felt the truly cruel sting that only skin on skin can deliver. It was a loud spanking. Alex had resigned himself to the fact that those in the neighboring hotel rooms or passersby in the hallway outside would most definitely hear the cracking report of each spank. But this wasn't a time to worry about what other people thought. Nor was this a time to accommodate the needs of others. He did enough of that in his life. This was time for him to demand similar respect. How dare she? How dare she leave without a word? How dare she make him feel like she did, make him worry that he had done something horrible?

Sarah couldn't know what was going through his head, but every time she thought the spanking couldn't get any worse, it did. Was this a just punishment, the equivalent in physical pain of the emotional pain that her leaving had caused, or was this just the satisfaction of that desire that had laid in wait, deep inside them, for as long as they could remember? What sort of calculus figured the amount of corporal punishment that equaled noncorporal pain? How big a debt had she incurred that she was now paying off in the currency of her own agony? Whatever it was, this wasn't what she had imagined. This was too much. This was too, too much.

She couldn't take it; she *had* to take it. These two feelings together had caused an initial panic but had subsequently settled into a feeling of deep resignation. She could rail against it in her head, but she did nothing about it. He spanked her again and again. It would go on forever, and each time she felt the vicious impact—each one worse than the last—she just struggled to breathe and make it to the next one. And the next one and the next one.

She was surprised when he stopped without warning. Was he done? Had she made it? Was that all there was to it?

"What's it like, Sarah?"

After remaining mostly dry-eyed through the vicious beating, Sarah heard the question and began to sob. Her tears came from a part of herself that she never let out. These were feelings—despair, weakness, hopelessness—that had to be kept inside or it would all fall apart. But the searing pain had defeated her, and she could hold it together no longer.

"This is what it's like," she managed from between her sobs. "This is what it's always like."

Alex was moved by the effort it took to say the words twice and knew that it was the first time she had been able to tell anyone the truth in a long time. He helped her off his lap, and she curled up on the hotel bed without pulling up her panties. He lay next to her and held her as she cried.

After a while, she faded into a deep fatigue, lying still, unconcerned about her state of undress or where she was or who she was with. This was unusual for Sarah, who typically worried about everything, and it came as a welcome relief. She would sleep well tonight, even without the pills. First, though, she had one question for Alex.

"Did I get the role?"

"Of course, my dear. Of course."

ALISON TYLER

THE GAME

G UESS WE'RE THE LAST ONES TO GET HERE," Angel said, as we pulled up into the driveway of Deleen DeMarco's Hollywood Hills estate. "That's good. You'll get to know everyone in about five seconds flat—then you can stop trembling and enjoy yourself." I nodded and gripped her hand.

It was, without a doubt, a trial by fire having to meet the entire band at one time. But, honestly, I preferred it that way, plunged into the group without a chance to step back, to move away from the flames.

Still, I was scared. I tried to control my nerves as I slid off her Harley, then waited while she set her gloves and helmet on the rack. We parked her bike in the circular driveway, already filled with other, more decadent bikes, and walked past them to the front of the house.

As a model, you'd think I'd be used to meeting celebrities—especially since I'm considered one myself. But I was fairly new on the scene. And meeting the members of Objects—the band with the most number one hits in recent history—was disconcerting, regardless of how many fashion shoots I'd done.

Angel pulled me along behind her, whispering assurances to me: "You'll do fine. They'll love you." We brushed past the multicolored balloons that filled the entryway, lolling against the molded doorways and fluttering softly up to the ceiling.

A poster of the new album, *Objects of Desire,* was taped to one wall. It showed Angel, Deleen, Beauty, and Arianna totally nude with Keith Haring–style arrows pointing to their breasts and cunts. Lola, the cherub of the group with her blonde ringlets and innocent smile, sat naked in her wheelchair, staring up at the rest of the group.

As I looked at the picture, I realized how each band member derived power through individuality. Angel's tattoos were starkly severe in the black-and-white photo, as if they'd been carved into her body. Arianna had painted stars and stripes on her breasts to make them more patriotic. Deleen was like a mad sorceress. She winked at the camera with an almost evil smirk and rubbed her hands together with glee. Beauty, who's half German and half Native American, had braided her thick, black hair into a solid rope—it made her look dangerous and mean. She stood sideways between Deleen and Arianna, and her braid hung down her back, past her shoulder blades, almost to her waist.

"That's the uncensored version," Angel told me. "The public receives a model with black *X*s covering the indecent parts."

I stared, fascinated by the curves and dips of the women's bodies, their unique shapes, but Angel pulled on my hand, leading me into the sprawling living room. The lights were dimmed, and I almost stumbled over a white cat walking up to greet us.

"Hey, Shazzam." Angel picked up the kitty. "I'd like you to meet Katrina."

I shook a fuzzy paw, and Beauty, lying on a red sofa said, "Where are your manners, Angel? You introduce your lady to a pussy before us?"

Angela shrugged, set Shazzam gently on the ground, and said, "Everyone, I'd like you to meet Katrina. Katrina, this is everyone." She looked around the room, "Well, almost everyone. Where are the hosts?"

Arianna, reclining on a matching red-leather chaise longue with her girlfriend said, "Somewhere in the kitchen." She was covered by a petite Asian beauty named Sara, draped casually over her like a shawl.

"You should check out the spread," Beauty told us. "Tessa got the Sleeping Buddha to cater."

Angel and I turned as Tessa appeared in the doorway, caught beneath the iridescent light filtering through a gathering of balloons. Tess is a true Irish redhead, her ivory skin sprinkled with millions of freckles like golden confetti. They seemed to sparkle across her nose and shoulders and over her cleavage, and I wondered if they covered her entire body, then blushed at the thought.

Deleen came up behind her, carrying a glass of champagne in each hand.

"Hey, Angel. Who's the babe?"

"Deleen, really," Tessa admonished. "You're frightening her."

"This is Katrina," Angela said, her arm behind me, pushing me toward them. I shook hands with Tessa. Deleen, passing the champagne on to Arianna and Sara, took one of my hands in both of hers and kissed my fingertips.

"Charmed," she smiled.

"Help yourself to food," Tessa said, ignoring her flirtatious lover. "We've got a feast spread out in the dining room, buffet style."

Angel and I piled up plates, then walked back into the main room and settled onto the floor against a flood of satin pillows. Tessa came to sit by my side. She had on a strapless dress with a black bodice and a short skirt of fluffy lace. Her slender waist was accentuated with a wide velvet ribbon. I complimented her on the look, and she said, "Thanks. Easy on, easy off," and then leaned across me to ask Angel a question, rubbing her breasts slightly against my knees.

I wondered if she'd done it on purpose, and then looked at her as she startled me with a question.

"I'm sorry, what?"

"Do you know Lola?"

"No. I know *of* her, but we haven't met."

"She should be here later," Tessa said, looking at Angel to include her in the conversation. "Lo was meeting with a publisher in New York about doing a book of photos. They say she's the next Herb Ritz." She paused, as an idea came to her. "You know, she ought to take some of you."

"The two of you together," Deleen interrupted. "Now, *that* would be a picture."

I saw Angel nodding in agreement, then I turned when Arianna leaned up on the sofa, Sara moving with her lover's body as if she were another limb.

"Add Sara, too," Arianna insisted.

"And, um," Beauty fumbled as a gorgeous strawberry blonde strolled in from the kitchen holding a bottle of mineral water. She walked up to Beauty and snuggled against her.

"Liz," she purred.

"Yeah, and Liz," Beauty finished, lamely, and the rest of us laughed, transforming an awkward moment into a rather silly one. Liz didn't seem to mind. She curled her long limbs around Beauty's, protectively, like an owner.

"I wouldn't get too comfortable if I were her," Tessa whispered to me. "Beauty left her last girlfriend on the plane when she met this one." Tessa nodded at Liz who was now kissing Beauty's earlobe. "Beauty's always had a problem with the word *commitment*."

Angel excused herself then to get more food, and Tessa took this opportunity to lean even closer to me. Her body pressed against my side so that I could feel her fragile ribs; the warm, bare skin of her upper chest on my arm.

"How long have you two been hiding out?" she asked. "We haven't seen much of Angel since the recording ended."

"A month," I told her, thinking that it was thirty days exactly since she'd come with Melanie to the fashion shoot at *Zebra*.

"And you met…"

"Through Melanie Samuel." I waited for the recognition to appear in Tessa's eyes.

"The journalist?"

I nodded.

"You're on the cover of *Zebra* this month, aren't you?" she said, getting it.

I nodded again, giving her a quick version of the smoldering look they'd had me do for the shoot—the one currently appearing on every newsstand. Lashes lowered, head tilted, lips pouting.

"You seem different in person," Tessa said, smiling at me. "So much younger."

"That's the makeup," I explained. "But it's what Angel said, too. It's what she liked about me, I think, the person beneath the image."

Angel had said, "Can I talk with you?" And I told her, knees trembling at the thought of talking with Angela McMorrow, lead singer in the hottest band in the country, "Hang out until I get this makeup off." She'd waited outside the dressing room, chatting with Melanie, who kept yelling for me to hurry up. I came out in a T-shirt and ripped jeans, my normal attire, and Angela looked me over and shook her head.

"You're younger than all that, aren't you?" she asked, glancing toward the lights and the fancy dresses hanging from a metal pole in wardrobe. "I'm the same age underneath," I grinned. "You just have to look beneath the surface."

Angel had nodded, moving in close to me as Melanie withdrew to answer her cell phone in private. "Yeah, I would like to do just that, Katrina. I would like to see what's lurking beneath your surface, peel you open, spread you out, learn each of your secrets for myself."

Then Melanie had returned and things continued as normal—at least until the next time Angel and I were alone. Still, I didn't say any of these things to Tessa. She would know all about duplicity, two-faced worlds, being the partner of Deleen DeMarco—someone whose little black book contained the number of every "in" person in Hollywood.

Angel came back then, now sitting on Tessa's side, and she gave me a look over Tessa's head that I took to mean, "How are you holding out?"

I shrugged back at her and then said, "Please," as Deleen stopped in front of me with a fresh bottle of champagne. It surprised me at first that there wasn't any help at the party, but I was glad for it, glad for the low-key atmosphere. I could tell that these people were for real—not needing the constant stroking of fans or media.

The house—mansion, really—was as kickback as they were, set up for comfort, not appearances, although all was stylishly done. There were pillows everywhere, velvet and satin striped, with butter-soft leather sofas. I hoped to decorate my own place in a similar fashion someday, wanting to be able to walk into a room, eyes closed (or blindfolded), and enjoy the surroundings by touch alone.

By my third bubble-filled glass, I was leaning against the cushions, listening to Montage croon on the stereo, drifting in a warm fulfillment. I paid scant attention to Angel and Tessa, who were discussing the promotion for *Objects of Desire*. I watched as Arianna and Beauty gossiped across the space between their sofas, Sara describing her latest nude centerfold in *Planet X* magazine, and Liz, a first-class cabin attendant, explaining how Beauty had stolen her heart at 32,000 feet.

I wondered what had happened to the girl Beauty had been with, and I thought about asking Tessa, but she left to fetch a joint. When she returned to the living room, she was tottering on her spangled high heels.

"Want some, Angel?" she asked, collapsing on the pillows on Angel's left side, turning my lover into a "person sandwich" with Tess and me the bread.

"Naw, I'm saving my voice."

"Katrina?" she asked.

"Sure."

Marijuana goes to my head quickly, especially when I'm drinking, so I only took one hit. But Tessa apparently had been smoking in the bedroom before coming out. She was flying, and while I lit up, she leaned seductively against Angel and said, "You have the most beautiful eyes, Angel. You know it?"

Angel tried to brush her off nicely by saying, "Deleen's the one with the killer eyes." Angel turned to me. "Did you know that Del's eyes have no color?"

I was more stoned than I'd thought, because this statement tripped a string of bizarre images in my mind. "What do you mean?" I finally managed to ask.

"They're almost perfectly clear. She usually wears shades or colored lenses to hide them. Del!"

Deleen looked over from her lazy-lioness position in the hammock chair.

"What's up?" She was gone, too.

"Come show Kat your eyes."

"Send the kitty over here."

I got up, also a bit unbalanced, and wove my way to Deleen's corner. She turned a floor lamp around so that the light shone directly in her eyes, and I drew in my breath. They were like glass, perfectly clear irises with liquid black pupils in the center.

Deleen smiled at me and said, "I always wear contacts for public appearances. I wouldn't want to scare anyone."

She put her hand out to steady me. I'd been rocking in place, and her fingers were like flames licking at my skin. Startled, I stumbled back to the pillow corner. Tessa was now in Angel's lap, her dress hiked up to her thighs exposing the purple ribbons of her garters as she straddled my lover. Angel didn't seem uncomfortable, but I could tell she was humoring Tess.

"You don't mind, do you, Katrina?" Tessa grinned at me. "Angel has the most inviting body. I wanted to be closer to it."

"Go ahead," I said magnanimously as I leaned against the wall, letting it support me as I slid to a sitting position. "Do what you have to." I wanted to see how far Angel would take it, wanted to know what I'd be in store for in the future. At the moment, she seemed to be letting Tessa call the shots.

Deleen got up to open another bottle of champagne, and I saw a frown on her painted lips.

"What are you up to, Tess?" she asked, her buzz obviously worn off. Deleen's demeanor surprised me, considering how she'd flirted with me when we'd met.

"Just goin' for a ride," Tessa slurred, leaving no doubts that Angel was to be her horse.

Deleen clicked her tongue against the roof of her mouth and then sat down on the nearest sofa, forcing Arianna and Sara to move aside. They protested for a second before resuming their positions: Sara had undone Arianna's leather pants and was very quietly sucking on the strap-on dildo that Arianna wore in a harness. The darkness of the room had concealed their activity, but they didn't seem to mind being revealed. Arianna's moans and Sara's kittenlike suckling noises testified to that.

"What is it with you, Tessa?" Deleen's voice was very softly menacing. "It's been three hours since you last came—is that too long for you?"

Tessa looked at Deleen through clouded eyes. "I'm just entertaining our guests, Del," she said.

"Uh-uh, baby, I'm not going to play that game." Deleen slid her hand through her silvery hair, apparently trying to calm herself down. Deleen's hair is completely gray and has been since her teens. She wears it combed off her forehead, and it falls like an old lion's mane straight down her back. "Get your little ass over here."

Tessa stood up quickly, a worried look replacing the lecherous one she'd worn only a second earlier.

"Now," Deleen ordered, when she saw Tessa hesitate.

Angel watched the whole scene with her features set. She appeared emotionless, a statue, but I could tell she was getting turned on. I was already able to read her expressions, the slight wrinkle in her brow or tightening of her jaw. I settled against her, and she put an arm around me, gently turning my face to kiss my lips.

Tessa cautiously walked the rest of the way over to Deleen, as if condemned. As soon as Tess was in reaching distance, Deleen grabbed hold of her waist and threw Tessa over her lap. Tess struggled, realizing suddenly what her Mistress meant to do, but Deleen held her firmly, scissoring one leg over Tessa's two squirming ones to keep her in place. Deleen lifted Tessa's dress by the hem, pulling it up to reveal a lavender lace G-string and matching garter belt.

"Katrina, would you mind bringing me my Harley gloves?" Deleen asked me, her voice unreadable except for the power in it, the command. "They're on the table in the entryway."

I looked at Angel to see if I should, but all she said was, "Go ahead, Kit-Kat. It's Del's party."

When I stood up, Deleen added, "Oh, and get me some K-Y, too, won't you? It's in the bathroom cabinet—the one in the hall." My heart racing, I left the room, gathered the tube of gel and the leather gloves, and walked back to Deleen, who still held the upended Tessa over her knees.

"Thanks, sweetheart," Deleen said as I handed her the items. I turned to sit down next to my Mistress again, feeling weak and confused. Angel pulled me to her, positioning me between her legs so that I could feel the wetness that pulsed through her jeans.

Deleen slipped Tessa's G-string down her thighs, but left the garter and hose in place.

"Better calm down, Tess," her voice was hypnotic, and I realized suddenly that everyone in the room had turned to see what was going on. Sara and Arianna, after struggling into semi-upright positions, were watching intently. Liz and Beauty, who'd been up to something on their own plush sofa, were now mellowly regarding Tessa, Beauty softly explaining to Liz how Tess and Del's relationship worked. I heard Beauty say, "Don't worry, Lizzie, it's just how it is."

Deleen had her worn leather gloves on, and she squeezed a generous supply of the jelly onto one finger and then spread Tessa's asscheeks with the other hand. Tessa continued to fight, but her slight frame was no match for Deleen's more powerful build.

"I said calm down, Tessa."

Although Deleen hadn't raised her voice, there was a note of danger in it, one that made me sure that if I were in Tessa's position, I would be still. Tess must have sensed it, too, for she was suddenly quiet, yet I could tell her muscles were tensed to escape if Deleen gave her the chance.

"Tessa wants to come," Deleen said, addressing the rest of us as a group for the first time. "She has an insatiable appetite." As she spoke, she worked the K-Y around and into Tessa's asshole. When she slipped a gloved finger inside her naughty lover, Tessa started to protest again. Deleen put her lips close to Tessa's ear, but we all heard her hiss, "Once more, baby, and I'll get the studded gloves."

Now Deleen had two fingers inside her and moved them in and out with increasing speed. She used her thumb on Tessa's clitoris, and Tess moaned, an obvious sound of pleasure that set off titters from Liz and Sara.

"Like that, don't you?" my Mistress whispered to me, and I nodded, leaning against her, feeling the hard synthetic cock that she was packing beneath the soft denim. Angel put both arms around me protectively as we continued to watch Deleen's progress with Tessa. Del was making her come slowly—bringing Tessa close to climax, then teasing her down. When Del had forced three fingers into Tessa's asshole, Tess started to move against her Mistress, fucking Deleen's gloved hand, working her body on it, but Del would have none of that.

"Tessa, don't," she said, a warning in her voice. It was obvious that Deleen did not want her lover to take any form of control, and I could tell that it took every ounce of Tessa's strength for her to follow this command.

"I'll make you come in my own sweet time," Deleen promised, before turning her attention to me. "Katrina? Tess was…" she cleared her throat before saying, "*riding* your property. Would you like to be the one to punish her?" She paused to look at me before continuing. "Because as soon as she comes, she's going to need to be disciplined."

The blood drained from my cheeks, and I turned immediately to Angel for help, but my Mistress shook her head, leaving the decision up to me, *testing* me, I thought. Flashes of conversations with Melanie replayed themselves in my head. "Leather," she'd said. "Bondage and dominance. Sex games. Wild, wild parties."

"I couldn't," I whispered.

"Another time," Deleen said, letting me off with a reassuring smile. Then in a completely different voice, a darker voice, "Did you hear me, Tess? You'd better try to slow it down, because I'm going to spank your little bottom as soon as you come."

Tessa started crying, and I knew it was because she was close to orgasm. And because, humiliating though it might be to come in front of everyone, being spanked would be worse. Deleen continued finger-fucking her asshole and stroking her clit. I noticed how gently she stroked Tessa there, and understood that Beauty was right, that despite what Deleen had said, this was a game, with Tessa a willing player.

And then, with everyone's attention focused on her, Tessa flushed, closed her eyes tightly, and let her body finally respond to Deleen's attention. She arched her back, tense with concentration, and came in a series of powerful shivers, electricity running through her body.

The room seemed lit by her energy, a shower of metallic sparks, alien green and copper, vibrating in the air. She was truly stripped, as if Deleen had peeled her layer by layer, leaving a nude and shimmering soul for us to see.

How awesome it must feel to be that free.

ABOUT THE EDITOR

C ALLED "A TROLLOP WITH A LAPTOP" by *East Bay Express*, Alison Tyler is naughty and she knows it. Ms. Tyler is the author of more than twenty explicit novels, including *Learning to Love It*, *Strictly Confidential*, *Sweet Thing*, *Sticky Fingers*, and *Something About Workmen* (all published by Black Lace), as well as *Rumors*, *Tiffany Twisted*, and *With or Without You* (Cheek). Her novels and short stories have been translated into Japanese, Dutch, German, Italian, Norwegian, and Spanish.

Ms. Tyler's short stories in multiple genres have appeared in many anthologies as well as in *Playgirl* magazine and *Penthouse Variations*.

She is the editor of *Batteries Not Included* (Diva); *Heat Wave*, *Best Bondage Erotica* volumes 1 & 2, *The Merry XXXmas Book of Erotica*, *Luscious*, *Red Hot Erotica*, *Slave to Love*, *Three-Way*, *Happy Birthday Erotica*, *Caught Looking* (with Rachel Kramer Bussel), and *Got a Minute?* (all from Cleis Press); *Naughty Fairy Tales from A to Z* (Plume); and the

Naughty Stories from A to Z series, the *Down & Dirty* series, *Naked Erotica*, and *Juicy Erotica* (all from Pretty Things Press). Please visit www.prettythingspress.com or www.alisontyler.blogspot.com.